HEARING VOICES
SEEING THINGS

HEARING VOICES
SEEING THINGS

William Wall

Doire Press

First published in 2016

Doire Press
Aille, Inverin
Co. Galway
www.doirepress.com

Layout & design: Lisa Frank
Cover image: Liz Kirwan
Author photo: Harry Moore

Printed by Clódóirí CL
Casla, Co. na Gaillimhe

ISBN 978-1-907682-44-5

CONTENTS

For my sister Deena

PAPER AND ASHES

I got the death certs for the crows. I call them the crows. When someone dies they all come pecking. I got five. I came out of the office and it was still daylight, like when you come out of the pictures. I'm there blinking and looking around me and everyone is wearing T-shirts. I'm thinking there was a reason why people used to wear black, like you're obviously a widow and people show respect. I probably look like just a thirty-five-year-old woman with a handbag full of death certs. Except they don't know about the death certs, that's the whole point.

So I went down to the river. The sun was shining. My late husband liked water. I thought about his ashes, standing there. I thought, *Wouldn't it be nice?*

Would anybody notice? There was just this old tramp asleep on a bench with a bottle in a brown paper bag. Even if he saw. I looked down over the wall, and the tide was out, and I could just see a shopping trolley in the mud. That gave me a laugh. Then I started to think wouldn't it be even better if I left the urn in a supermarket trolley. Someone would find it and report it. Would the person who lost the human ashes please come to the information desk. Better again if I put him on a shelf. In the pickles section. Or in the fridge with the soups. If I could get one of those stickers. 'Reduced to Clear'. I remember my late mother saying once, That man of yours knows the price of everything and the value of nothing. Everybody says that about accountants.

So that's what I was thinking when someone hit me right between the shoulder blades. I don't remember falling out onto the road, but I remember the sound of a car passing right near me. I remember thinking, *That one missed me.* Then someone was helping me up. It was the tramp.

My death certs, I said.

No fear of that missus, the tramp said.

No, I said, they were in my handbag.

The tramp pointed up the street, and I saw the boy who hit me. He was running and throwing things. The things were from my handbag. Bits of paper. Keys. My mobile went over the wall into the river. Some of the death certs were going up on the wind. I could see one drifting over the wall. I started to run but my back and shoulders hurt. I had to stop. All of a sudden I had a bad headache. The tramp started to run too, and he got about three feet ahead of me. Now he was leaning on his knees wheezing.

We walked. We did not say anything to each other. I was thinking, *Why is this tramp walking with me? We're like an old couple.* When we reached the place where my bits started, I found my car keys.

I saw the certs going upriver. The tide was coming in. They were just floating. Now how am I going to prove he's dead?

The tramp looked at me.

It's just paper isn't it? he said.

My late husband, I said.

I liked saying *late.*

I'm sorry for your trouble missus, the tramp said. I found myself shaking his hand. I never touched a tramp before. I let go as soon as he let me.

My credit cards, I said.

My late husband would have thought about the cards first, then the phone. He wouldn't have bothered about the certs. All I had to do was go back into the registry and queue again and they'd give me out a hundred if I wanted them. It was stupid.

Suddenly I thought, *I have only this old man.* Even at the funeral they were all laughing behind my back. Those that aren't owed money.

I had the ashes in the boot of the car. It was in the car park. I could be back in five minutes. If we tipped him into the river he'd go upstream with the certs and end up in a bog somewhere. He'd have his papers anyway. Or stuck in the bank. He might even drift up some disused sewer and spend the rest of his days hoping nobody would flush. From what the solicitor told me, that's the way he'd lived for the past two years anyway.

At that moment I felt on top of things. It was the end of a stressed-out week. Waking up in the morning and finding your husband dead in the en-suite is no joke. He had his pyjamas down around his ankles.

What's your name?

Saddam Hussein.

I stared at him.

My mum called me after my old dad, didn't she? he said. That was before he was famous.

Is that true?

No. I don't give out names. I got issues, see.

Can I call you Saddam?

He grinned. His upper false teeth fell down, and he closed his mouth quickly. After a bit of chewing, he said, Lost them before that way.

He moved away from the river wall.

I'm going to be gone for a bit. If I come back will you still be here?

That's my bench, he said, pointing. Unless it's raining I'll be over there under that stairs.

I went to the police station first. I told the duty officer about my bag. He wrote it all down. He let me use the station phone to cancel the credit cards. He asked me if I had a witness. I told him about the tramp. He sighed. That's not a witness, he said. Name? Saddam Hussein. It did not go well.

I went to the car park. The ashes were under the passenger seat not in the boot. I remember putting them on the floor. They must have rolled.

So what do we say?

The tramp looked at me. Then he composed his face in sorrow and joined his hands in prayer.

For what we are about to receive we thank thee Lord, he said. No that's not right, he said. Hang on.

I could see he was thinking because he was chewing. I suspected he was moving his upper false teeth around. After a bit he coughed and then coughed again and said, Man that is born of a woman hath but a short time to live, and is full of misery. He cometh up and is cut down like a flower; he flieth as it were a shadow, and never continueth in one stay. In the midst of life we be in death.

I stared at him. I was crying. Where did that come from?

C. of E., he said, my old dad was a vicar, wasn't he?

Your old dad was a vicar?

Why I don't go in houses see, I got issues.

Because your dad was a vicar?

Oh yes.

My husband left me penniless, I said.

The tramp nodded at me. I like a nice chat, he said. Get things off my chest. It's good that.

But he looked worried. He took a step backwards. He held his hand out low and flat like he was patting a child's head.

Idle hands, he said, get on with it.

I was still holding the urn. It was surprisingly light. Is that all we come down to? I was thinking this was better than he deserved. My late husband, accountant, investor extraordinaire, hopeless case. Maybe it was better than I deserved myself. I remembered a time when we were courting. Down here at the river. We had a cardboard box of Colonel Sanders' Kentucky Fried Chicken. I could identify the actual spot a few hundred yards along the quay. A crow and a seagull were arguing over something. We ate the chicken facing each other, sitting on the wall like people sitting on horses. I met him at a disco. He was a smooth talker. The tide was in that time. And it was the night. I confess I was happy to have hooked a fast talker, a man with ambition. I remember he explained the stock market to me. Greasy kisses too.

Chuck it in missus, the tramp said. Get on with it.

He pointed at the urn. He was agitated, I could see that. He didn't like me changing my mind.

I don't want to.

Now he was shifting from foot to foot as if he was running on the spot, but he wasn't lifting his feet. He was looking around him. There was a thread of spit on his chin. Then he said, Discipline discipline, discipline, that's what makes a man, self-discipline yes. We had a nice house. We had a disused tennis court.

Your dad?

We had a flush WC, didn't we? He used to come in my room very late very late and examine the sheets. 'Forgive, O Lord, for Thy dear Son, The ill that I this day have done.' What if I fell asleep? Where was my mum you ask?

He walked away. I watched him going along the street. He was still talking. He was waving his hands. I could see he was arguing. He didn't sit on his bench. He turned a corner. I felt I had let him down.

The sun was sinking behind buildings.

I opened the urn. It was a screw-cap. I tipped the ashes out, and the wind took them up. The ashes were a pale yellow colour. There was a man on the other bank watching me. He blessed himself. The ashes blew out along the river and the tide carried them upstream. They were headed for the country. Paper and ashes. Like someone had thrown a fire away.

I BOUGHT A HEART

I bought a heart. It was a sheep's heart. I intended to stuff it with bread, onion and thyme. It was raining outside but the market was covered. My jaw was killing me. It hurts more on wet days. The butcher was watching television. There was a small screen set on the wall to the left of the counter. Look at the fuckers, he said. Jimmy, I said, you shouldn't say fuckers to customers. Sure you're hardly a customer at all, he said, all you buy is fucking hearts, Jesus, if I was depending on you for a living. He pointed at the television. Look at the bastards, after screwing us for ten years and now we're supposed to feel sorry for them. The sound was turned down. Do you know what I heard this morning? he said. Did you ever hear the expression stockbroker sentiment? Sentiment my arse. Put me down for two hearts next Thursday, I said, I'm expecting company. He wrote it in his book. Then I went away. I did not have an umbrella. I walked as near to the wall as I could because it's drier there. There are awnings overhead from time to time. I thought about a quick pint but realised I didn't have the money. The heart broke me. My mother is coming out for the day on Thursday and she still likes hearts. This is something I don't understand. She doesn't know my name. She doesn't recognise me. She doesn't remember that she has a child. But she still likes the taste of meat. She even remembers that she likes the taste. I sometimes think that the stomach has its own brain. When the rain got lighter I made a run for it. The pain in my jaw stopped when I ran. That's a good one, I thought, if I could keep running I'd never get pain any more. But you can't. Running would kill you quick enough.

Crossing the bridge the heavens opened. It was that straight down rain. It came down under my collar and through my clothes. I stood into the doorway of the funeral home. The rain made the river smooth. Then it stopped and in a minute the sun came out. That was when I noticed that she was behind me. She was crying. Are you all right, I said. Look, I said, I have a heart. She just looked at me. I'm going to stuff the fucker, I said. I don't know why I said fucker. I suppose that was Jimmy coming out in me. Jimmy is a big influence. Even when we were kids my mother used to say you were out with that Jimmy Canty again, the tongue he has, I can hear him in you. The woman came forward. What kind of a heart, she said. Sheep, I said. I'm going to stuff it. Lovely, she said, do you cook yourself? I do. Good man, she said, I'm all for that. I said, Did someone die on you? My husband, she said. I'm sorry. No, we were estranged, I haven't seen him in a while, he's in there now, I just thought I'd nip in before the new family arrives and say goodbye, funny thing is I never cried when I said goodbye before, I suppose I'm sentimental. Is he open for viewing? I said. I don't know, she said, I didn't go in yet. I'm just sheltering from the rain. So I see, she said. What did he die of? A stroke, at his age, you wouldn't expect that, would you, except he was a workaholic of course, that can't be good for you, he had no life. I said I could go in and have a look at the corpse with her. She looked at me without saying anything for a bit during which time it started to rain again. Then she said, Would you? I said I would. We went in and had a look. We had to ask someone in the office because there were three corpses in three different rooms. He was lying in a nice-looking coffin with silk lining and what I thought were probably gold-plated handles. He was stone dead and he looked it. I saw the way my father looked.

People said he looked beautiful because all the lines in his face were gone but I preferred him with the lines. They said death took forty years off him. That was no good to me because death took everything from me. We ticked gold-plated handles on the menu the undertaker gave us. We ticked hardwood. We ticked marble headstone. We gave him everything but when he was in a hole in the ground, nothing made any difference. He was just gone. Everybody said it was a great send-off. That didn't make any difference either. I said that to the woman and she said it didn't matter to her because the new family were paying for it, she wasn't even notified except a friend saw it in the deaths. She started crying again. That was the way he looked, she said, he was a handsome chap, he was gorgeous really. Then she spat in his face. She did it twice. Missus, I said, what are you doing, you can't do that. That's for everything he did to me, she said. Then she said to the corpse, How do you like it now you fucking dead bastard, much good your fucking fancy woman did you. Come on, she said, I need a drink.

She bought the drink. I told her how the heart took my last euro. I'm totally stony, I said. God help you, she said, so am I but at least I have the price of a drink. Where there's an undertaker there's a pub. I asked for a pint of Guinness and she bought it for me. I don't know what she was having herself because she mixed it at the counter. It looked like a glass of water with ice in it but it wasn't. In my experience women like vodka and gin and you can't see either of them. She told me the story of her life. It was quite interesting. The relevant part was where her husband came home one night and she could smell the other woman on him. She went ballistic. Totally ballistic. Up until that minute they had never had a serious row and since then she often thought that it was a bad sign. If they had rows, it meant they would have something to fight about. Did he admit it? He did eventually. What did he say? I can't remember, that's the kind of thing you want to forget, it wasn't nice, what did I ever do to him, I ask you? She went up and ordered another Guinness and another glass of invisible alcohol. I saw my orthodontist come in. As soon as I saw him the pain in my jaw started all over again. The glass of water had a little Chinese umbrella in it. So, I said, what are you going to do? She drank half of her glass. When she held the glass up the Chinese umbrella slid against her mouth. The removal is in ten minutes, she said, so we have to get ready. Then she finished the rest of the glass and went for another one. She came back with a whiskey for me and another umbrella glass. Down the hatch, she said. There was something like a dead smile on her face. I said, That man is my orthodontist. What do you want an orthodontist for, I thought you were broke? I had major reconstructive surgery, I said, after an accident. Down the hatch, she said. We drank our shorts together. I cycled into an articulated lorry, I said, I was coming down the hill, he backed out, to tell you the truth I wasn't looking. Jesus. They fixed me up in the hospital and then they sent me to him. He identified an overcrowding problem. He screwed up. He's a crap orthodontist.

I said, I'm going to tell him he ruined my life. When I stood up I was a bit shook. I'm not used to drinking so fast. I sat down again and finished the whiskey. Come on, the woman said, I'll go with you. We went up to the orthodontist. Excuse me, she said, this gentleman has something to say to you. But I couldn't say it. I just stood there. I wanted to say, After what you did to me I can't hold down a job. I got fired because I was sick and now the company is gone too. He didn't recognise me. Orthodontists probably only recognise teeth. I opened my mouth. I tried to open wide but the joint doesn't work a hundred per cent anymore. He looked away. I could see he was embarrassed. I can't say I blame him, this fucker with a wired up jaw opening and closing it in your face without saying a word. He probably thought I was a maniac. He may or may not have remembered something. He pretended to be looking at the news. It was Sky. A line along the bottom said, Fed buys AIG. Jesus, he said, this is big.

Come on, the woman said, it's time for the removal. She pushed the orthodontist's arm which spilled his drink onto the counter, You ruined his life, she said. Then we went out and saw that there was a respectful crowd at the door of the funeral home. Right, she said, don't let me down now.

I said, I left my heart in the pub.

Fuck your heart, she said, come on. She pushed through the crowd and I followed. It started to rain again. We turned in the door and I saw the coffin ahead. I could see that her shoulders were shaking. I thought she was probably crying or getting very mad. There was a priest and a young family. I could see the new wife.

She looked beautiful the way sorrowful people do. There were people in suits. There was an old woman who looked like my mother. She was looking at us. I could see she didn't know what was going on and she wasn't happy about it. I tried not to look at her. In my mother's world now something terrible was always going to happen. Even in her bed in the Home she was fretting. There wasn't enough of her left to be happy and happiness is the only defence against fear, I know that. I saw the same thing in that old woman. I couldn't do it then, whatever we were going to do. I turned around and went out.

My heart was still where I left it but the orthodontist was gone. I went home. There was bread there, and onion and thyme. When it was cooked it was delicious. I watched television all evening. I remember exactly what was on.

FOR FUN TIMES PHONE DODGER

I saw a note on the back of the toilet stall that said For Fun Times Phone Dodger and a phone number for a cell phone. I had a twenty-four-hour stopover, so I thought what the hell. I called him up on the payphone. May I speak with Dodger, I said. And half an hour later we were shaking hands. He was not at all the kind of person I expected. He seemed restless and slightly hostile, but I saw that there was an essential light-heartedness in him that had led him to write a note on the back of an airport toilet door about fun times, and so when he proposed buying a bottle of whiskey and taking it back to his place, I assumed that there was no whiskey in his apartment and that he needed some. I could also see that Dodger was not very well-off and it is an article of faith with me that poverty does not make for fun times.

The first place we went into refused to sell us the whiskey and so he suggested that in the next place I should go in alone as very likely they knew his face. A bottle of whiskey is an expensive item in Ireland. In his place he suggested that we take all our clothes off and get relaxed. The whiskey tasted good after my long flight and in a little while I felt the fun times begin inside me. But Dodger did not seem to be having fun. His apartment was typical of the urban poor and the toilet and kitchenette were not clean. The television was on all the time and it was the news. It was about how they sentenced Saddam Hussein to death. I didn't like it so I asked him to turn it off because I had enough bad news to last me a lifetime. He did turn it off. He asked me if I had shares and I said shares in what and he thought that was funny. His room was painted red and when I suggested that red was not a fun colour he said, Oh so you're a fucking interior decorator, are you? I said no, I was not an interior decorator. Well, he said, you sound like you come off a different fucking planet. I saw that as well as restlessness, hostility and light-heartedness there was also anger in him. He was looking at me and, I thought, trying to figure me out, which is not hard, but the whiskey was clouding his judgement and it made him look like a comic book spy. This made me giggle and he asked me what I was giggling about and I said I was having fun. This did the trick. He cheered up and put his arms around me and said if I would see him all right he would do anything for me. I could see him all right, he was just standing there, I couldn't miss him. But he said I didn't understand, he needed money. I asked how much did he need. He said two hundred would do the job nicely. What job I asked him and he said he needed to fix up the flat and get the room painted. I told him I would give him five hundred because interior decorators are always more expensive than you think. He jumped up and asked me was I serious and I said I would write a check there and then. He said I should get my clothes on and go down to the ATM and get it in cash because if he presented a check at the bank they would simply hold onto it in part payment of his overdraft.

So I got the money out of the ATM and he said we should buy some coke and celebrate but I said I do not do drugs and was not interested in hanging out with someone who did drugs and he said of course I was right. So we went back to his place again and took all our clothes off and he was really having fun. He thanked me several times and kissed me for it, which was a strange sensation as you do not expect to get a kiss from a man when you do him a good turn. Then he started touching me and

I was really embarrassed and said I had to go to the toilet. In the toilet I took stock of the situation and decided that my new friend might be gay and maybe I should put my clothes back on.

When I came out, I found it hard to find all my clothes. Dodger kept following me around the room asking me what I thought I was doing and I kept trying to say I was looking for my clothes but my voice was very slow and I felt quite dizzy. Then he stopped me looking into the kitchenette by putting his arm around me and touching me down there in such a way that I got a giant hard-on. He was behind me and he started rubbing himself up against me. I saw what he was up to and told him that I didn't want any homo stuff and he asked me what the fuck did I want and I said all I wanted was fun times and he said what the fuck did I think he was doing and I said he was touching me up and it wasn't fun and he said what the fuck did I want and I told him again.

By now he was doing something behind that I thought might lead to unpleasantness and so I broke free and went into the kitchenette. I said to him you are a homo and he said what did I expect and I said I already told you, Dodger. I could see that as well as restlessness, hostility and anger, there was also fear in him. He went out of the kitchen and I took the opportunity to take stock of the situation again. I decided that the whiskey was having a very peculiar effect on me. I was hungry and looked around for something to eat but all I could find was a loaf of bread. I cut three slices and ate them very quickly and after that I did not feel so dizzy.

While I was eating I could hear Dodger talking to someone on his cell phone. Everybody raises his voice on a cell phone. I found my underpants under a chair and started to get dressed and then there was a knock at the door and a girl came in. She talked very nicely to me. She said I was a very attractive man and that she could see we would get along very well and that I would be nice to her. You will be nice to me, won't you, she said and I said I liked to be nice to everybody. But especially to me, she said. Right on, I said. She was a very nice person and she had a smiling face but inside her face I could see she had the same qualities as Dodger. She asked me how I liked it. I said I liked it fine and she laughed. She asked me would I like her to get comfortable and I said I would and she said I didn't look very comfortable in my clothes and would she take them off for me. I was dizzy again and I sat down and she took my pants and underpants off and started to touch me and kiss me and Dodger was watching, which I did not think was polite. I said you shouldn't watch and he said if I didn't like it, it was fine with him as long as I was happy. But something about the way he said it suggested to me that he didn't mean it. I said he was lying and he said I should lie back and enjoy myself. I got the girl to stop. I couldn't remember her name even though when she came in Dodger said this is my mate X. She said how did I want it and I asked what and she said what the fuck was I up to and she didn't do any funny stuff. And Dodger said I gave him five hundred and she whistled and said she was extra. I said I was up to my limit. By now I was getting seriously worried that something was going on. She said get his cards off him and let's fuck off, and Dodger said she should keep her mouth shut and she said couldn't he see I was some kind of spa and let's get the cards off him and do a runner. I said I didn't have any cards and the two of them started to laugh. And what's all this so, Dodger said holding up my wallet and showing me the three credit cards my old man gave me when I started my trip.

I noticed that there was a wart on the side of his groin just above his pubic hair that didn't look too good. He was always scratching it. This was a really characteristic gesture that I will always remember him by. The wart was bleeding slightly. He said he was taking my clothes and locking me in but he'd be back in about an hour and I could have it all back including my cards. He said he would take my cards for a walk. But he didn't come back in an hour and all the clothes in the wardrobe were too small for me and anyway they were not my style. I fell asleep and when I woke up it was daylight. There was no phone in the apartment and the door was made of aluminium. I had a terrible headache. I ate the rest of the bread and drank the milk that was in the carton in the fridge. Later in the day I got hungry again but there was nothing left. I opened the window and looked out but the apartment was three floors up and the street below was very quiet. I decided to keep the window open and look out from time to time. I shouted at a woman going by with a stroller and three plastic bags. She looked up at me but she didn't say anything. I said I was locked in and someone had gone off with my clothes and my money, could she call the police? I asked for the police because it was obvious that whatever was happening was wrong. There must be a law against this kind of thing. Nobody should be legally allowed to take away your clothes and your credit cards and your money and keep you locked in an apartment three floors up. The woman went away and after that any time I shouted at someone they just hurried on and didn't look up. It was getting dark about eight o'clock. There was a drainpipe quite near the window. I got out and knelt on the window-ledge and I was just able to touch the drainpipe. If I let go of the window and tilted slightly I would be able to catch hold of it and slide down. Then I heard voices inside the apartment. I got back in but I found that the voices were outside the door. I listened. Someone was talking to me and someone else was giggling. We're coming in now, the voice said. I knew it was Dodger. Don't be pissed off now, the voice said, we're coming in, OK? We have nice prezzies, OK? Here we come. I heard the key in the lock. Then the door opened and what a transformation. Dodger was wearing a smart suit with a silk shirt and the girl was wearing a long evening dress that made her look quite something. You really look something, I said. Well, thanks, she said. Champers, Dodger said, and paté, and a take-away, look. We brought all this stuff. I want my clothes, I said. They giggled. She came over to me and kissed me and started to rub me but I didn't get any hard-on this time because I was angry and restless and hungry. I said I have to catch a flight right about now and they said never mind the flight. Dodger popped the cork and the champagne flowed out over the floor. I noticed that they locked the door when they came in. I said I want my clothes. Sandra give him the clothes, Dodger said. She gave me a bag and I saw that there was a silk pyjamas in it. I said I can't go to the airport in this. Sandra said, Tell him the news. And Dodger said, We got a balance on your card, there's twenty thousand in that one, the one you used earlier. I said how did you get my pin and then I remembered how I got the money out and he was standing by my shoulder. We're keeping you here for a bit, Dodger said. We're going to have fun times and you're going to have the time of your life. Like I'm going to do everything, Sandra said, anything at all you want, you won't be sorry, I'm going to do whatever you want, just tell me whatever comes into your head. Absolutely, Dodger said, me too. Your wildest dreams like. So I went into the kitchen and I got the bread-knife. Take it easy now, Dodger said. We'll give you back the clothes, but you'll be really missing out. I said get the clothes now and he said they were in Sandra's flat upstairs and I said get them and the two of them went for the door. No way, I said, Sandra stays here. Dodger tried to grab the knife and when I pulled it away it sliced his palm. There was a lot of blood. OK, he said, Jesus, oh shit. Sandra got him some tissue from the toilet. I said, leave the keys. He gave me the keys and he went upstairs to her flat. I could see that there was a lot of fear in Sandra. She was crying too. Dodger came down and gave me my clothes and the credit cards. He had something tied around his hand. Look, he said, no hard feelings like? I said I believed he and Sandra were not bad people but they got carried away by money. I said what my father always said, that wealth was something you needed to respect. They nodded their heads in agreement. I put the knife down and got dressed. I didn't let them get near the knife, but they didn't try anyway. They just stood there watching me. I could see that the restlessness and the anger was gone but I couldn't decide what took their place. When I had my clothes on I felt better. Got to get going, I said. Probably missed my plane now. I would need to get my stuff out of the left luggage. Before I closed the door I took one look around the apartment, just so I could remember it exactly the way it was. Actually these experiences are priceless.

UNEDITED TRANSCRIPT RE. FEAR

I would like to express my sympathy to the family on behalf of myself personally and the theme park company in these difficult financial times, and the Ghost Train operator who is gutted. Nothing like this has ever happened here in the last twenty years since my company took over the running of the theme park. We are essentially a property company and what we do is we rent space to rides to be operated on site. The rides are all licensed by the appropriate licensing authority and we have no involvement in that. All the rides at Happy Garden are fully compliant with industry health and safety regulations, but accidents do happen. If you could cover everything, there would be no need for regulations at all, but you can't, which is why we have health and safety, to prevent this kind of thing. Which makes something like this all the more upsetting for everyone concerned and we would like to express our sympathy with the family of Timothy Doran who was taken from us at so young an age, which is tragic really. The Ghost Train operator is completely gutted. He is fully compliant and is a member of the Showman's Guild in Britain and also has international experience.

But all the experience in the world wouldn't prepare you for someone to be decapitated in your ride. I'm saying decapitated but of course we have to await the results of the post-mortem but I was one of the first on the scene and I can tell you it was decapitation all right. I know you can't print that, that's off the record now, but it was like a battlefield in there. Except of course there is no evidence of any altercation I hasten to add. I'm talking about the blood and the remains. The remains were like something out of *Terminator Three*. I would like to express my sympathy in particular to Mr and Mrs Doran who I know quite well. Frankie Doran was captain at the golf club there last year, as you know. My heart goes out to them and to all the family. We're all totally in shock.

As far as we can gather the incident took place in the Horror Cave section, which has a narrow entrance which is essential because it is pitch black inside, and it looks like there was some leaning going on, that's off the record, I quote what our insurance rep said when he looked at it, but that's only a first base position, we'll have to wait until the health and safety people make a full report. We're holding our hands up and saying let's wait until all the report is in and then we'll make a full statement.

At the moment we're in a state of shock as you can imagine. Especially as the little boy was handicapped, which we have a brilliant record on. All our rides are disability friendly and the whole site was revamped three years ago to comply with best practice internationally in the industry, ramps everywhere, full wheelchair accessibility, even though I know the wheelchair issue wasn't an issue on this occasion, but just to show that we've been responsive to the general area. Happy Garden are proud to say our record is second-to-none on disability issues. Which makes it all the more harder to take.

Mr and Mrs Doran are heroes around here for people like me, the way they fought tooth and nail for that little boy is nothing short of heroic. We were all behind them all the way. The people around here are the kind of people that get behind someone like that, we're the kind of people who are there when you need us. I don't have kids myself so I'm not well up on the school end of things but if you ask me it's a disgrace that someone like Tim Doran has to go away to a special school when all his mates are going to the local school, there should be provision for handicapped kids because, let's face it, it's hard on the other kids in the class, and of course the teachers, if you have someone disruptive who is handicapped and inclined to be disruptive through no fault of his own, which basically means the Government is way off on this. I'm a member of the party myself locally, as you all know well, but I'll hold my hands up and say that we're way off on this one and we should never have fought that case. You have to make provision full stop. Mr Doran whom I know quite well personally, he was the captain in the golf club, was down here the time he was running for the Council and he was fully consulted on all the changes and, as I understand it, he personally took the Ghost Train ride at the time and enjoyed it. He was a big fan of the theme park; he told me he used to come here himself when he was a kid and he used to sneak down to the slot machines with the pocket-money when the mother wasn't looking, which, you know, a lot of local kids still do; it's amazing how these things carry on from generation to generation.

Mr Doran was an excellent captain I will say that, and although he was elected as a single-issue candidate and effectively acted as a spoiler against our man and put him out for the first time in sixteen years, there's no hard feelings, that's politics and the electorate is the ultimate authority; but I have a feeling he'll be unseated again next time out. The party always wins in the long run and the single-issue candidate finds it very hard to keep the steam up going forward. We're already on a war footing now in the party, getting ready for the next round, but I'd say Mr Doran is still trying to find his feet.

Anyway, I digress, as the man said.

What I was going to say was, we used to have Timmy down here often with his brother. Now I can't say I knew him well, only just to see him around. The Ghost Train operator knew him all right and I understand he has stated that he refused him entry on several occasions for health and safety reasons, which I fully understand and which he is fully entitled to do; the legislation entitles him to refuse entry on health and safety grounds, which nobody is claiming was any kind of discrimination; this park is second-to-none on discrimination. Nobody has ever claimed against us, not even coloured people; we have several coloured operators here, the Bungee Slingshot operator is Nigerian and we have several Lithuanians. Our policy on employing non-nationals is straight down the line, we make absolutely no distinction full stop. I would like to knock that on the head straight off. The Ghost Train operator was concerned for H&S reasons and the legislation entitles him to refuse entry on those grounds, which, as it happens, he was justified when you think about it. I mean if he stuck to his guns this time wouldn't we all be better off? But you never really hear about the successes which happen every day, when the health and safety checks and balances do what they're supposed to do; it's only just the one time that it doesn't work that you get in the papers and you people come out. But if you reported the good news stories all the time, I suppose nobody would open the papers at all. But I would say frankly that the pressure on the Ghost Train operator was fairly intense to allow Timmy into the ride after the complaints and the pressure from the Council.

The ride was of course fully compliant as such and any normal person would have known not to lean out, in fact the Ghost Train operator always specifically mentioned that people should not lean out, or try to get out from under the safety bars, or try to exit the cars during the ride, or climb up on the cars, or try to make contact with the ghosts or in any way interfere with the smooth working of the ride. There's a full notice to that effect, but, I suppose, you know, little Timmy was different to that, you know, and we'd be relying on his brother who accompanied him to restrain his actions, but I suppose it's a kind of a tribute to the ride itself that the brother was terrified, I mean that's what the Ghost Train ride is all about, isn't it?

So it looks like this is all just a tragic event that should never have happened.

I'd like to take this opportunity to express our sincere sympathy to the family of little Timmy Doran on behalf of myself and the company and the Ghost Train operator as such. I would like to also say that last year we ran a whole week when we had collection boxes at every ride in aid of the Society for Autism and this was in response to requests from Mr Doran. So we have been responsive to the general area and, as I already said, a few years ago we revamped everything for wheelchair accessibility. We would be holding our hands up here and saying it obviously wasn't perfect, but there's full transparency and accountability and we'll be making all our plans and specs available to the inspector. But I will say this, no company in the industry has done more for accessibility than Happy Garden. This theme park operates to the highest standards in the industry in these difficult financial times.

So allegations of negligence will be fought all the way, we don't accept negligence and we'll be making this plain through the court process going forward. We don't want to see this ending up in litigation that might take years and could work out badly for all concerned, and we'd like to extend our sincerest sympathy to the Doran family in this terrible time for them and to assure them of our fullest sympathy. All we ask is for Mr Doran to refrain from making unfounded allegations against the Ghost Train operator. We have a clean sheet as regards health and safety and needless to say we'd all prefer to have kept it that way, but Mr Doran's allegations are unhelpful at this time.

So we'd like to make the following statement re. the unfounded allegations that have been circulating since yesterday: one, the train was travelling at the normal speed as specified and there is no way of altering the speed at the control box; two, the safety bar was in place and checked by the operator as usual and there is no way of lifting the bar while the ride is in progress; three, the ghosts do not interact in any way with the passengers, they only appear, make noises and gestures and disappear again, they have no remit to interact directly with anybody on the trains and if any ghost is found to have interacted this would be against company policy and will in no way be defended by the company if an action is taken; four, there was no misalignment of the track and further the company denies that any such alleged track misalignment would be sufficient to bring a passenger's head in contact with the scaffolding to which the outer wall of the ghost cave is attached; five, any alleged remarks made by the Ghost Train operator are hearsay and given the operator's vast international experience and his membership of the Showman's Guild unlikely to be proven, but should any remarks be proven to have been made in regard to poor little Timmy's mental problems, this company will in no way stand over that; six, the company and the operator jointly and singly deny that the word *freak* was specifically used by anybody at any time in relation to the deceased, or that such words have ever been used in relation to anyone with mental or physical shortcomings by any of our operatives or other employees and that any allegation of such use of the word *freak* will be vigorously defended in court if need be; finally, the shouting heard by the other passengers is part and parcel of the Ghost Train experience which is to generate fear for a short period of time during the actual ride. The motto for the Ghost Train ride which is painted on the side is *Max Fear* and our Ghost Train is second-to-none in this regard. However, our notice to passengers specifically warns anyone with heart problems not to get into the Ghost Train and we always advise passengers to read the full terms and conditions, and going forward we'll be updating this notice to take account of this tragic event in consultation with our legal people and the appropriate medical authorities.

But I will say this, some people don't understand fear. I'm not talking about specifically people with mental problems as such, it could be anybody. But we're not allowed to specify mental problems on a public notice. You'd never be able to put words on that one. I mean you can't say only normal people can go on the ride.

Fear is a natural part of our lives as you see every day now, passing through airports and so on. I'm winging it a bit here, but what I'm trying to say is little Timmy Doran was not able to fully partake in the fear like the rest of us and quite possibly he panicked unnecessarily and tried to get out. He might have easily thought the ghosts were the real deal, not seeing things the same way as the rest of us, you know. As far as

I understand the situation, he would be what they call high-function which means he was not subnormal but the other way round to be honest. As far as I can gather at this point it's fair to say that shouting and the use of obscenity might be part of his condition and, given that he might have thought the ghosts were really after him in some way, he might have directed his obscenities at them rather than at the operator, which might also explain why he would have tried to exit the train in the course of the ride. Which would explain why the other passengers heard threats which they thought were directed at the operator even though they couldn't see anything in the dark. I will say the ghosts are completely shocked by the whole thing and a few of them are out sick today, which doesn't affect things anyway because the ride is closed for the duration.

So in the circumstances I think we should all take a rain check until the dust settles on this one. Nobody should be making unfounded allegations against anybody. In the meantime, the Ghost Train is closed until further notice but all the other rides in Happy Garden are operating as normal. As the man said, the show must go on. You can pick up your free passes at the office. Enjoy.

TORCHING SAM

Right outside Sasha Hair & Beauty was the little shit with that slut from Lidl. I could not go in. I walked. After that I was like kind of off. My room is still totally messed up, so I texted him and told him I want his shit out and I want my ring back, it belonged to my mother. He called me back, I saw SAM on the screen. First I thought no way, he can text the answer and then I thought might as well, what the fuck. He was like, What ring, girl? What ring? The fucking ring I gave you the first night we made it together, what else? I don't remember no ring. You fucking bastard return it to me. I was crying. I said, All you do is disrespect me like I'm some kind of scumbag. How do you think I feel? Anyway it looks like the ring is no joy, so I'm going to sell his shit. Let's see what he thinks of that.

So after the call I'm feeling kind of yeah. I ring Natalie but she doesn't pick up. I make up my mind to do Sam.

I ring Natalie again.

This time she's there. She says, Don't let him mess with you, Tori, you need to stand up for yourself. So I'm like, Get your sorry ass over here, Nat, I need you to be there for me. Next thing I know she's on the buzzer. She got a taxi.

She gets into bed with me and we turn on the TV. It's the nine o'clock news whatever. It's all about bombing places. So I get a DVD out of Sam's shit.

It is *I Am Legend*.

We have a laugh right there. Wrong again boy, I say.

Then I'm crying. Where did that come from? I'm like totally weeping, like I'm gutted. She touches me. You're all cold, Tori.

I tell her I need a good shag. It's so long now since.

Don't look at me girl, she says.

That was another laugh.

Well we watch *I Am Legend* and I get pizza in. The pizzas are OK. We open a bottle of vodka I got from my Mum. She's always forgetting where she leaves the drink.

And Natalie has blow.

So we nozz up and do some vodka and watch *I Am Legend* again. The second time round it's way better.

Four in the morning Nat says we are the lezzer avengers and we're going to torch that shit fucker and Sandra the slut.

We don't know what we could torch them with. We need assistance.

Natalie has money so we get a taxi to her place. We hook up with Natalie's brother Jake who is up for doing something usually. Usually I stay away from that crackhead.

When we tell him what we're doing he doesn't want to be there.

Let's just go get faded somewhere and kick it, Jake says.

I just know he has his eye on me. If you think I'm going to do you, you fucking chief wanker, you can forget it.

Jake is like, Aw come on, Tori.

So we get in his car and he drives round for about an hour, trying to find someone with something and, in the end, we finish up outside

Sam's house and the only idea left is torching. So we scope out a few Bud bottles under the front seats and that, and Jake has this tube for sucking petrol out of cars, like he never actually bought anything mostly, and he fills three bottles from his tank. I have to admit he's cool at all that. I am attracted to cool.

So then the subject comes up about rags to stuff into the bottles to make petrol bombs and Natalie shouts knickers. It is brilliant.

We get in the back seat and get our kit off with Jake hanging out trying to see in. He gets a good look at mine. I don't think there is anything to not like. It even crosses my mind, I might do him later if this works out. Then he gets his knife out and we cut the panties in four and stuff them into the bottles. Like it was an ordinary penknife. I expected something more like on telly. But to be fair Jake is really into it. The buds and that. He is laughing.

I make a speech before we get to attack. I say, You guys were always there for me, I'll never forget it, now let's go torch the fucker.

Jake lights one of the bottles. It is nice like a picnic and even it is beginning to drizzle.

But Natalie starts to cry totally ruining the whole atmosphere. She sits down against the side of the car. I don't believe I'm doing this, this is illegal, we'll all go to jail—that shit.

Well, I say, what about nozz and that? Nozz is illegal too. You shoulda thought of that first. Right now I need you to stop living in Natalie world and be there for me, cool?

Jake tries to get her up. Come on Nat, don't be like this, don't be crying, sis. He accidentally like kicks over the burning bottle and the ground catches fire in leaks. Natalie says she definitely is not up for torching Sam. Cool by me, I say, what we'll do is we'll just leave bottles outside his door and knock and run away. He'll come out. He'll see the bottles on fire. He'll get the message.

What message is that? Jake says.

Like he can't mess me around, I want my ring, like hands off that slut bitch.

Cool, Jake says.

Natalie says, I'm not going up, Tori. You go up.

And Jake is not up for it. I'm trying to think where he could have popped something. I never saw anything. That wanker has all sorts, he keeps it to himself. He is moving sort of sideways and his hands are hanging out from his sides. His right knee is bent all the time. I think he is going to flip over. He looks like one of those ducks that suddenly get their ass up in the air. Swans whatever. I was with Jake once. And I thought he was getting kind of attached and the sex was bomb, of course, but it was not to be in the end. We were only there for maybe a week but it was OK. Then I worked out how bad he was, he never treated me right and when he did, it was like whatever. Tori, see if you can get a slab of beer, Tori, I'm hungry, Tori this and Tori that. He tried to get me away from my mother where I was living at that time. He said your mom is a total case, no way is mothers meant to be stoned night and day. Well he was right about that as I eventually discovered. In counselling.

Give me the buds, I say. I'll fucking do it myself.

So I take the two last buds upstairs. I'm real careful like I didn't want the stuff to leak on me. I'd be a right spa with hands on fire knocking on the shit's door. Lucky enough I don't meet anyone on the stairs. I know Sam's flat number 219. The two means second floor.

I tip the buds over to wet the panties.

I light the panties.

I put the buds down outside, like I said.

I am so careful.

I knock. There is no answer so I knock louder. I'm like, Come out before the fucking bottles blow, aaaasshole.

He doesn't come out. I start to get mad.

Then the door opens and this pervy old dude looks out. He is wearing a stripy pyjamas like you see.

Who the fuck are you? I say.

He sees my buds. They are smoking. He panics.

Oh no, he says.

Oh fucking yes, I say.

Please, he says, what do you want?

I want Sam.

Sam who?

Aw fuck off, I say.

Right there I knew god was on my case, no way was he going to let me torch Sam. A long time ago my Mom said to me, You are going to hell child, God knows everything you do. Well I'm like thanks Mom it really makes me feel better.

I walk away. I just somehow know I had the wrong room. Now I'm thinking it maybe was 319 or 229. I look back when I get to the stairs and the old fart is trying to pick up the buds but he can't bend his back. Like old people can't bend their backs.

I shout, Fucking wanker.

I give him the finger on both hands. Old folks make me sick. They should just like die.

When I get down Jake is totally out of it. Natalie is laughing. I just know from the laughing that she got something from Jake. What had that arsehole up his sleeve? Nat, Nat, what did you get?

I'm shaking her hard.

I don't believe you're doing this to me, Nat. Right now I need you to be there for me.

No, she says, you torched him all right, I thought you wouldn't do it.

She's pointing up. I look up. I notice one of the windows on the second floor is burning.

Sweet fuck the fart, I say, he must have leaked it. Shit is right fucked up now.

Jake sticks his head out the door. What are we doing here? he says.

Nat says, She just like torched Sam's place.

Wrong Nat, I say, Sam is not 219.

Jake looks around him. I can see he's trying hard. Taking it in. He shakes his head.

The fire alarm starts to go off. Like why don't you get a fire alarm before you get a fire, instead of too late?

So we drive. I don't know where we drive. I'm still a tad off. I get horny too when the drink starts to go down. But there is nowhere to go. Jake wants me to come into the front and do him while he's driving. I keep saying I want Sam. I tell Nat I want Sam's kids but I'm sorry because she tells Jake and Jake starts this laughing like you hear in jungles. It creeps me out totally. I'm like, Ok Jake I'm good, no more laughing. In the end we drive out the beach, right down onto the sand and fall asleep looking at the boats and that.

It was sad. But sooner or later I know shit is going to change for me. I just know.

THE TRAP

It happened the day the Jesus-man called. I was alone in the house when I heard the knock. I opened the door and saw immediately what he was up to. I said, No thank you, I don't believe in God. You're the very lady I want to talk to then, he said. I stood there exasperated while he explained to me that I could have a free bible and for a small sum of money, sufficient only to cover the cost of printing and binding, a free reader's guide to the Good Book and he could call again and talk it over with me once I had read a little. The main thing I would discover in that there book was that Jesus loves everyone in the whole wide world.

Right, I said, come in and let's see what your god can do about this. I brought him into the kitchen and showed him the trap.

I saw immediately that he had seen the same thing as I had. The mouse had rushed into the trap and then become stuck in the glue. Its front paws were stretched forward and were glued down as far as the elbow-joint. Its chin was glued down. It had attempted to scrabble backwards with its hind legs. It looked like someone kneeling on a prayer mat.

While we were watching the tail moved. The tiny jet eyes watched us. Its upper jaw moved a little.

How is it going to die? the Jesus-man asked.

I tried to get one of the paws off, I said, using a blunt knife, but it's stuck fast in the glue.

It's going to starve to death, isn't it?

I can't bear it, I said.

I didn't tell the Jesus-man, but since I came downstairs this morning I have been sitting here in the kitchen watching the mouse. I had the radio on for a while but pop music does not go well with starving things. For the past hour or so I watched in silence. Every time he moved. And sometimes I could see his heart beating. Wondering how long it would take. It was a Professional Strength Victor Glue Trap. It worked.

You're going to have to put it out of its misery, he said.

I looked at him. He was a small man, but very well-proportioned, with broad square shoulders and a fine narrow head, a small blunt nose and small mouth, curly hair. He had placed his little bag of bibles and readers on the table beside the saucer of milk that I was planning to offer the mouse, until I noticed that his lower jaw was glued down too.

I never go out anymore, I said. I have anxiety. I worry about everything. I never sleep.

He was looking at the mouse. Why did you buy a trap like that?

It's more humane.

I only ever saw the ones with the spring.

They still die slowly.

He nodded his head. You're probably right.

What I want to know is, how is your God going to save that mouse?

He leaned back against the sink and folded his arms. His shirt was as white as ice. There was a knife-edge crease to his trousers. Did he do his own ironing? Was there someone waiting at home to know how Jesus went down today? I saw that he was more comfortable now. He didn't like looking at the mouse but he was happy enough looking at me and wondering what I'd have to say about Jesus. And what he could say back to me. He wanted to convert me.

The choice is yours, he said. God will not make it for you.

Why not?

God made the mouse and he made you.

God made the trap.

God does not make traps.

I said, Right come on.

I led him down the short corridor and into my bedroom. I showed him the bed with the sheets thrown back. I have no idea what I thought he'd see there or why I needed to show it to him.

Right, I said, I loved him. You understand that? I left my family for him. I came here for him. To this country.

I don't know what you're talking about.

What's your name? I pulled the wardrobe door open. The jackets were still hanging there. Four of them. Two tweed sportscoats, a Parka and a windcheater.

I'm sorry, I should have said. I'm Andrew. He held his hand out. I took it and held it. After a bit he took it away again. He was embarrassed.

These jackets, I said.

He looked into the wardrobe. What?

Want one? I'll give you two for a fiver.

Are you serious?

I laughed. I took out the two tweed jackets. They were what he wore to work. Where did he go? Maybe he got run over by a bus. Or fell in front of a train. Maybe I should go to the police and file a report. But I didn't want to go out. I ordered my groceries from Tesco. Every little helps. The truth was he got tired of me. I'm a wreck. I worry about everything.

The Jesus-man didn't say anything. I could hear his breathing.

Do you want the jackets or not?

He waved his hands. I recognise the signs of panic when I see them. He backed out the door. He backed down the corridor and, without turning his back on me, he reached for the knob on the Yale lock.

Ok, ok, I said, tell me about God.

But he slipped out. He did not stop on the outside. He went down my three steps, down to the pavement. He looked less physical. For a time, in the bedroom, as he walked backwards, I was almost frightened of him although he was clearly frightened of me. These irrational responses. People say, Get a grip. Get over it.

Standing outside my house, he said, Can I have my books back please? I left them in your kitchen.

I got his books. I threw the bag at him. It was a Marks & Spencer's Eco-Bag. Bibles and readers tipped onto the pavement.

Jesus loves you, he said uncertainly.

Fuck him.

I closed the door. Immediately I was sorry. I thought I should call him back, ask him to talk to me about being saved, about how to save myself. Could I be born again? This time as a different person? The corridor in front of me led directly to the trapped mouse. Now is the kind of time I would like to phone home but all that was closed to me. You burned your boats, my father said to me the last time. Just before hanging up. But he would know what to do. My father was a godly man in his way. He knew all the priests. He never hurt a creature but he hurt me. He was the kind of man you would call on to put an animal out of his misery. When our dog got cancer he took him away. I saw the shotgun under a rug in the boot of the car. I knew what was happening but I did not run after the car crying. I left him to his fate. He was lying on an old coat in the back seat. He was shivering, the way dogs shiver from pain. Even today I cannot say his name. But my father turned the key in the door against me. He shut me out.

I would not allow the mouse to starve to death in my sight. Even a mouse deserves a decent end. Even if I set the trap myself. That night when we were arguing, shouting at each other, telling each other lies for truths, I said to him, After all I've done for you. Immediately I knew they were my father's words. I was ashamed. At that point all I wanted to say was, Go if you must, but I'll be here. Why didn't I say it? Instead I repeated my old complaints. We go round in circles when we most need to see straight. We take the crooked way. As soon as the words were out of my mouth I saw the mouse. He skittered along beside the skirting board, then under the table, then past the leg of the kitchen chair and in behind the fridge. So I set the trap and we went to bed. And in the morning my man was gone. And today this poor bastard was glued to the floor.

So I tore a cornflakes carton and made a kind of shovel of it. I moved the trap onto the cardboard with my foot and I carried him out into the garden where nothing grew. The high grey walls of Shepherd's Bush. I put him on the path. I found a large stone. I knelt and said, Goodbye little fellow, I'm sorry, I'd let you go if I could, but I can't. I dropped the stone on him from high above my head. I saw that he was stunned but still moving, still awake even. I dropped it again and struck him only a glancing blow. Once more and I missed. Tears made me miss. And I was shaking. I found a bigger stone, a fragment of concrete from the top of the wall. It did not kill him. There was a loose slab at the end of the path. I prised it up and lifted it. It was extremely heavy. I raised it as high as I could and brought it down with force. When I lifted the slab away I saw that he was completely crushed. His brains were out, smeared on the glue and the cardboard, a little grey contrail from the jet of his head.

I went inside and found a shoebox. Yesterday I bought him Nike Air. He was so pleased. He appreciated small things but the restlessness always got to him in the end. I suppose I am one of those people whom it is impossible to love. A fearful, self-centred child, a hole in the heart, a solitary.

When I looked down at the little mouse I realised that even if I scraped him into the shoebox there would still be the smear of brains on the cornflakes carton. So instead I put the shoebox down over him. In time the creatures of the night and the soil would undo him. The glue would lose its power. Some day, in the not too distant future, the morning light would reveal a tiny beautiful skeleton at prayer.

I AM LOST IN THIS HOUSE

I am lost in this house. They said everything would be the same. My youngest comes every day. I am eighty-four years of age and my eyes are in a bad way. I'm used to myself. I lived alone since my children grew up. I buried my son. He was my second. It was a bad time then for all of us. Still we lived. They say the living live above the dead. And women live too long that's certain. But I have two sons in America and a daughter in London, I have four grandchildren, Mary my youngest is with me still. She comes every day. She got a flat herself. I don't know where anything is.

They knocked my house down.

She brought me back to see it but I'm lucky I'm almost blind. I can see sideways a bit. I looked straight at it and all I saw was light at the edges. It was a glorious day, I could feel the heat on my face. The last good day of the summer. My eyes are in a bad way but I hear everything. I can hear the neighbours fighting. I like things just so. They say when you lose one sense the others are stronger. I can hear them two houses up. I can hear mice in the attic. I don't think they're rats. I was born in a house in Blarney Street and we had rats in the attic. It was like the

Charge of the Light Brigade. These are mice. They will come down once the cold weather comes. I won't see them.

My mother was a cleaner and I had two brothers and four sisters. I was the eldest. She went out at five o'clock every morning to clean offices. She did the Munster and Leinster Bank, Nathan's the accountant's, Dwyer's offices and places like that. I was always late for school because I had to mind my sisters and brothers. I was the eldest of seven. I got murdered every morning for being late. I can read and write, well I could before I lost the sight of my eyes, but I learned it myself, I never learned anything in that school because I was always afraid. Old Dwyer left money in his will to build a steeple on the church. We called it Dwyer's Fire Escape. Good morning Bessie, he used to say to my mother. Her name was Elizabeth. She'd be scrubbing his floor. I'm lost in this house. I wake and if I can hear mice I know it's night and I'm upstairs. Sometimes I see shapes or people. I saw my mother in a blue gingham dress. She was floating. I knew it was not my mother because she never had a gingham dress. She wore black all her life and a shawl to cover her head. She was a widow and I am not. The doctor says seeing things is part of the eye trouble. My eyes are in a bad way. The head tries to make sense of the eye, he said. My youngest comes every day. When I lived in my old house I had neighbours. They said everything would be the same. We all know where old Dwyer went, my mother used to say. She meant Hell.

I came up here when I was married first and we had a flush toilet. That was my old house. I want to go back to my old house but it's not there. They knocked it down. I don't know why. My youngest told me. I didn't see it myself. I can see sideways a bit but I didn't look. It's the kind of thing you don't want to see. As a matter of fact I didn't want to go but she brought me. She comes every day. Only for her I'd never know anything. I am lost here. If I hear mice I know I am upstairs and it is night. My youngest has a car. She works for Apple. I don't know what she does. She tells me all the news. It was her who told me about my husband. He went to England when she was born. There was no work here. He was a mason. He sent home postal orders. The money was handy but it didn't last.

She says, He's sick, Mam. I says, He made his bed and he can lie on it. She says, He wants to come back. I says, He had some fancy woman, he left us. She says, He's still your husband and my father. Well, I'm not taking him back and I don't want to see him.

If he came back in a coffin I wouldn't want to see him.

All he was ever good for was making babies. And I had enough babies to keep me going.

He was always light on his feet too, a lovely dancer, and handy with his fists.

Mary my youngest says he has cancer of some kind. If he has I don't know why he came back here. He'd be better off in Dagenham. That's where he went. The place the batteries come from. I haven't seen that man in forty years and more. I will not see him now.

He'll be company for you, my youngest said.

I said I have the mice. If he has the Big C, he'll have to wait years for a doctor. We have waiting lists for the waiting lists here.

She says, He wants to die among his own.

That's Dagenham so, says I, for there's none belong to him here.

It was the first time ever I had a fight with my youngest. But still she comes every day. She cleans for I can't see it. My eyes are in a bad way. I was a terror for cleaning once. I got it from my mother. You could eat your tea off my floor. Now I can't see it. They said everything would be the same. But I don't know how to turn on the washing machine. I ruined my nightie and some drawers. I boiled the lot. I said to myself that smells hot. But I didn't know how to turn it off. My youngest had to go out and buy me another. You need a change. This house is not the same as my old house. My youngest turns the heating on for me. She times it.

She starts as soon as she comes in the door. Dad was saying such and such. Dad says this. Dad says that. He's living in her spare room but she wants him out. I warned her. You let him get his foot in the door and you'll never shift him. I said, He better not raise a hand to you. He was like that. He was a lovely dancer.

Dad says he wants to talk to you.

Well I don't want to talk to him. He said everything he needed to say when he stopped writing to me. It wasn't the postal orders.

Dad. When did she start calling him Dad?

But she keeps at me. If I keep saying no will she stop coming? I am lost in this house. A woman came and gave me an alarm I can feel. I'm meant to keep it around my neck. I don't like it. I don't like anything around my neck. I had five children. I buried my son. I don't like anything around my neck. My youngest put it beside my bed. I know it's there. If I wake and I hear mice I know it's beside me. Sometimes the mice are quiet. I just wait.

I buried my son, James my second, the year my husband left. It was the polio. Mary has a short leg. That was the polio too. It went through this place like the wind. We were all afraid. A priest said to me one time, The mothers carry the world on their shoulders. They do father, says I, with the priests on their back always with the hand out for dues. He didn't like that. It was only the truth.

Now it's Dad this, dad that.

I put my foot down. Much good did it do me.

I says, I will not have that man in my house, I don't care what he has. And it doesn't sound like cancer to me. He's down the bookies every day.

So, she says. She comes every day. She turns the heating on. My eyes are in a bad way. I see things sometimes. Seeing things is part of the trouble. He wants to make up with you, she says. He wants to put it all behind. It is all behind, says I, that's the point. She says he never had any fancy woman. I know that's a lie because a neighbour has a daughter in Dagenham. One of my old neighbours. They said everything would be the same but I don't know anybody here. I never see them. They're out to work by day, and by night they watch television. I hear their voices. Sometimes they fight. I don't like to hear it. The language is desperate. I am eighty-four years old. I like things just so. But I'm lost in this house. I don't know where anything is. I can't turn the heat on. I boiled my nightie. My husband can see, so Mary my youngest says. But I won't see with his eyes. I don't want him doing my washing, turning the heat on. I don't want to set eyes on him. Not even to look sideways at him. When he went to England Mary my youngest was eleven months old. What is he to her? A stranger from Dagenham. He came back to die. Let him die with his daughter. I'll die on my own. Or let him die in our old house. There's a space there for him. They knocked it down. I don't know why. I couldn't look at it. My eyes are in a bad way.

He knocked on my door this evening. The cheek of him. I was asleep. I woke up and I couldn't hear mice so I knew it was still day. After a while I heard the doorbell and I thought I was in my own house. My house is gone of course. Nothing is the same here. For a while I couldn't find the door out of the room. I could see a door but it wasn't a door. Seeing things is part of the eye trouble. Then I remembered where I was. I said to myself, This is not an old neighbour coming. Whatever possessed me I had the sense to put the chain on.

Lilly, he says, it's me.

He has an English accent now. It was a bit of a shock.

Lilly I'm not well. Can we talk girl?

I says, I still have the last letter you sent me. It's in a drawer upstairs. I'll get it and read it to you.

I can't read it of course. My eyes are in a bad way. But I know it by heart.

Please Lilly, I'm not well at all.

You said I'll be home in the spring. That was the winter. Now it's winter again. And forty years later.

That's all water under the bridge, Lilly.

It might be water under your bridge but it's not water under mine.

I never forgot you. I was always thinking about you, wasn't I? Every day I said, What's my Lilly doing now I wonder?

Do you think I forgot you? With five children under me? I'll be home in the spring you said. You said you were making good money on the buildings. Then you found your fancy woman.

He didn't say anything to that. I knew I was right. I buried my second the year after he left. That's something you never forget. My youngest has a short leg. It troubles her sometimes. We were all terrified of the polio. People stopped going out by day and by night. It was an epidemic, they said.

Go back where you came from, I said, for I don't want you.

Then he said, I was on the sick, wasn't I? I got three fingers crushed in a cement mixer, didn't I? I never made good money, Lilly. It was hand to mouth every day until I got in the Post Office. I was ashamed. That's it. I was ashamed to come home.

I thought I could hear the mice but I couldn't. It was something in my head. I am eighty-four years of age. What was I meant to do? I took the chain off the door. I like things just so but my eyes are in a bad way. He came in. He was always light on his feet. He tried to do something but I didn't let him. I'm not having any funny business.

This is nice, he says, very cosy.

They said everything would be the same, but everything is different.

How would you know, he says, you're blind as a bat.

I went into the kitchen and sat down. I know where everything is in here. I like everything just so. I don't want him moving things around to suit himself. I said, You let him get his foot in the door and you'll never shift him. My youngest said, He only wants to talk. I know the talk of him. To be honest, when he stopped writing I was just as happy. Mary was my youngest. She was not even walking when he left. What was he to her? A stranger from Dagenham. He went upstairs. The steps creak. He was always very light on his feet, a lovely dancer. And I was always afraid. Now I can't hear him. He'll be opening drawers. I'm used to myself. My eyes are in a bad way. I saw my mother in a blue gingham dress. She was floating. Maybe she has blue now, but she never had then. It was always black for her. Seeing things is part of the eye trouble. They say when you lose one sense the others are stronger. I can hear the neighbours fighting. It must be night.

SAY SOMETHING

I want my tablets. I say it to her but she takes no notice. She is talking to a salesman. The prescription is in her hand. She's not looking at it. I need it. She is a blondie. Blondies are like that. Miss, I say, Miss. She ignores me. I want to go round the counter so she has to see me but the girl from cosmetics is looking after the till and she's blocking my way. I do not want to get up her nose. The girl from cosmetics is nice.

She's busy right now, says she.

Miss, I shout, Miss.

The blondie looks at me. The salesman looks at me. There is a customer sitting on a chair. She looks at me. I look away.

After a while the blondie comes out with the salesman. She walks right past me. She goes out to the door. She stands talking at the door. The salesman lights up a cigarette. He's got one of those shiny suits. He has a briefcase. He has black shoes but the heels are not polished. The arse of his trousers is greasy from sitting in the car. I walk up to them. They don't look at me. After a bit I walk back to the counter.

They're out there chatting, I tell the cosmetics girl.

I know, says she.

I can't bloody believe it, I say. I need my tablets.

We look at them, the cosmetics girl, the other customer and me. The salesman lights up a fag. Blondie says she doesn't smoke. I cannot hear her but I know what she's saying. She doesn't even like the smell of it. She steps back.

Smoking kills, I say to the cosmetics girl.

I know, says she.

The other customer asks, Will it be much longer? I have to put the dinner on.

Hey Miss, I call. Miss!

Blondie turns towards me. She puts her hand on the salesman's arm. Then she takes it away. She comes in and she walks right past me without so much as a word. After a while she comes out with a prescription but it is for the other customer. She takes her over to the side of the counter furthest away from me and they get their heads together. They are talking about the prescription. I can hear even though they are trying to be quiet. I have excellent hearing. It is about an infection in the you-know-what. Apparently she should drink a lot of water. No matter what they give you, you have to drink a lot of water. The prescription always says, drink water. Or eat food. Take with food. This medication may cause drowsiness. Or dizziness. Sometimes it may cause the very thing you're taking it for.

She goes back into the pharmacy part. She comes out again. She has my prescription in her hand.

Mr Rice, she calls. She looks around in case there's someone else called Rice waiting for his tablets. Then she looks at me. This is out of date.

I look at her. She can see I'm mad. I've waited all this time.

I can't dispense this, she says. It's two months out.

I'm trying to think what to say. I feel the tears coming. Lately my bladder has been very close to my eyes. I want to say something that will change her mind.

My tablets, I say. I need my tablets all right.

She shakes her head. She gives the cosmetics girl that look. The cosmetics girl looks away.

Another customer comes in. She goes straight up to the counter and holds out her prescription.

Excuse me, I say.

Oh sorry, the woman says.

It's OK, the pharmacist says. She takes the woman's prescription and goes into the back.

Hey, I shout, what about my ruddy tablets?

The new customer steps away from me. It's like I'm going to hit her or something.

The cosmetics girl says, Now Mr Rice, don't be upset.

At that moment I cry. It's because the cosmetics girl is so nice. I turn my face to the wall and try to get a grip. It is not easy. I feel very stressed. Things are going against me. The cosmetics girl hands me three tissues. They are menthol scented. I blow my nose and feel my head clearing. I didn't know it was blocked. Maybe it was the crying. All those tubes in your head. Who knows what goes on? You get sinusitis. And migraine and dizziness. They are called the Eustachian tubes. There are other things too, I forget what.

I'm dizzy, I say to her.

Sit down Mr Rice, says she. She takes my arm and pushes me sideways. I sit down hard on the seat. Put your head down, she says. I feel her hand on my neck. I put my head down on my hands. She takes her hand away. In a minute she comes back with a plastic cup of water.

I sip the water. She squats down in front of me. She looks concerned.

It's that bitch, I say. Where's the nice Polish girl you had last month?

Shhhh, says she. But I know she agrees with me. She looks towards the blondie when she says it.

Is he all right, poor man, the new customer says. She is fat.

The cosmetics girl pats my hand. He's a bit dizzy is all, says she.

I can't see straight, I say.

The new customer laughs. My husband says I'm beautiful because his sight is going. He never said it when he could see me.

The cosmetic girls laughs. That's a good one all right.

He never said it at all when he could see me.

The two of them laugh.

I stand up.

Will you stop that for god's sake, I say. Give the man a bit of respect, not to be laughing at him in public.

Excuse me, the fat woman says. She takes a step away from me.

Now Mr Rice, the cosmetics girl says.

I want my tablets, I say. I go towards the counter but the girl is there before me.

I'll ask the pharmacist, says she.

She goes into the back part. I can see blondie in there. She has her arms folded. She's leaning against the shelves. She's red in the face and her mouth is like a pencil line. She must have heard everything.

Hey blondie, I call, give me the tablets.

She turns her back on me.

I hear the two of them talking. I hear the cosmetics girl say recently widowed and blondie turns around to look at me. I just hate that look. I'm not putting up with this. I have rights. I'm going to give her a piece of my mind.

I lean across the counter and point at her. *This place is...*

I'm shouting. I can hear myself. I'm trying to think what it is.

...it's fucking antediluvian.

I turn around and walk out.

There's a bus waiting at my stop. I walk straight on. I show my card and sit down. As the bus pulls away I see the cosmetics girl. She is standing in the doorway of the pharmacy. She is looking at me. She has big sad eyes. She gives a little wave as I pass. I wave back. Then, I don't know why, I blow her a kiss. She smiles suddenly. If only there wasn't blondie. They had a nice Polish girl.

I forgot my messages. I have to go back to the SuperValu. I have nothing in the house.

At the next stop I get out. It's too far to walk back but I don't want to go home. I'm thinking if I could get back and talk to that girl. I cross the road and sit down at the going back stop. I don't know when the next bus is coming. Then this kid walks over. He has all this hair down over his eyes. I feel like telling him to straighten his back. He has his earphones in. He sits on the bench at the other end. I think he's looking at me.

What's wrong with you, I say.

He cannot hear me because of the earphones. Kids these days are away in their own world. But he'll end up in my world just the same. That's life.

There is a woman waiting for the cars to stop so she can cross the road. She wants the bus too, I'd say. She is an old woman. She's older than me. She looks across at me. I get the feeling she can't see me because when I nod at her she doesn't nod back. But she looks away all right. So maybe she does see. She has shopping bags. I think I know her face from somewhere. She has bad legs, I can see it from the way she walks. Her feet are sore.

I going to have to go back to the doctor, I say to the boy, to renew my prescription.

He still says nothing.

The doctor won't give it to me though, will he?

The boy gets up suddenly and moves outside the bus shelter. He stands with his back to me. If the bus comes he won't even see it.

Hey, I say, hey.

He doesn't move.

I can't fucking sleep, can I?

I notice that I'm shouting again. I swallow down whatever it is that's in my throat but I still want to shout. I do not care anymore. That's what I think. I am beyond caring. The kid starts to walk away. Now I know he could hear me all the time. Why didn't he say something?

The woman crosses the road.

Now it's raining. What next? It's bucketing, missus, I say. Come in out of the rain. She sits down beside me. They won't give me my tablets. The prescription is out of date.

That's awful, certainly.

She's a nice woman.

I haven't slept a night since my wife passed away, I tell her. I miss her in the bed. I can't get used to it.

My fella is gone this ten years, she says. And to tell the truth, I don't miss him at all. Would you believe that? He was always complaining. I like my own company. Do you ever play a hand of Bridge? It's a great pastime.

The bus arrives. Surprise, surprise. I let the woman on even though I was first at the stop. She says, Thank you. The boy with the music comes running. He gets on behind me but there is no seat left. Serves him right. I am sitting beside the woman. I hold out my hand. Michael, I say. She says, Betty. Everyone calls me Mike. Everyone calls me Betty, she says. We have a right old laugh at that. Are you going or coming? I say, pointing at her bags.

I'm going into the Copper Kettle for a cut of their chocolate cake. I can't resist chocolate cake.

Do you know what, I say, I'm gasping for a cup of tea.

JOHN AND MARY 1995

I found the ring on my way home from mass. Inside it said John •Mary•1995. It was outside the Polski Sklep shop, so I went in. I said did they have a customer called John or Mary?

They did the shrug thing. They said they didn't know.

I said I found a gold ring outside. They looked at the ring.

The big fellow said he didn't know anything about it but I should go to the police but the police will just keep it of course. The small one said I should go down to the shop that buys gold and sell it. He was the son. The big one was the father. Or at least that's what I thought. But now that I think about it, there was a different small one there before. The big one turned to the small one and said something in Polish. The small one looked away. He was upset, but I could see he was only joking when he said about the We Buy Gold shop. I smiled at him and he looked at his father. Or the big one anyway. I went out.

It was a fine day.

I thought about it. I tried the Leisureplex but no one even talked to me. I play the slots there. It is my pastime. I walked down to St Peter's and knocked on the priest's door. It was the black priest who came out.

I said, I found a ring and it was owned by a John or a Mary and I know they were married in 1995. I was wondering if you could look up the register and see who owns it.

The black priest just looked at me. Then he said he'd get Father Harkness. He asked me to come in. This was my first time in the priest's parlour. They had a lot of uncomfortable chairs.

Father Harkness came in but the black priest came too. Father Harkness sat down beside me. Father Harkness said, So tell me, Packie, what's troubling you?

I told him I found a ring and it had John and Mary 1995 on it, and John and Mary must be gutted, whichever one lost it. I showed him the ring. I explained to him that he could look up the register and find out who owns it and I could give it back. He said it mightn't be that easy. They could have been married anywhere, Packie, they might live in a different parish and come down to shop here. This is a big city and there's a lot of people called John and Mary. And even if I did look up the register there could be ten of them in 1995. Or maybe they moved since then.

I said I had to give it back.

Father Harkness told the black priest that I was a good man and a daily communicant. Was that supposed to be bad? I don't see what business it was of his. Father Harkness said to me that I was getting a touch of the scruples, that I was only required to make a reasonable attempt, that I should put up a notice in the shops and the church, someone would be sure to see it. And if nobody came I should keep it for a year and then it was mine. I never thought of the notice. He asked the black priest to get a sheet of paper and a pen and when he brought it, Father Harkness wrote out the notice for me.

Found

A Ring

Please call

17 Girvan's Buildings

If not in, leave name and address

I liked it. They photocopied it in their office. The blackie gave me Sellotape.

So I went down to the Polski Sklep and they let me put it in the window. I put it in the window of Extravision. I put it in the window of the Fryer Tuck.

I had a portion of chips and sausages because it was my dinner time.

I put it in the window of the bookshop.

But the We Buy Gold crowd wouldn't let me put it in their window. The man was quite rude. We don't advertise other people's gold, he said. Even the hotel let me put up a notice on the door but when I came back later it was gone. Probably the manager saw it. The girl was nice. She said it was awful to lose a ring like that. She said she knew a John and Mary and she thought they might have been about fifteen years married. She gave me the address and it wasn't far away.

It was up the hill. The girl didn't sound like she came from up the hill.

I went up.

I don't usually go up because it's a rough area. The people up there are mainly trouble my dad used to say. My dad could look after himself. He was handy with his fists. So the last time I went up it was for a funeral. I forget who died but it was someone old. It was a massive funeral. I found the address where the girl said it would be and I knocked on the door. It was the Mary who came out. She was a bit of all right.

She had on a white T-shirt and skinny pants. You could nearly see everything.

I said I found her ring and she looked at her hand straight away but there was a ring on it.

She said it wasn't her ring.

She showed me the hand with the gold ring and the diamond ring. It was a very small diamond. I asked her her husband's name. It was John. I said did she get married in 1995 and she said she did. I said that was weird.

Then she put her hand to her mouth. It might be my husband's ring, she said, but he never wears his. It's too small for his finger.

My dad said they are terrible liars.

She asked me could she see it. I said I couldn't just show it to her. She'd have to tell me some identifying marks. She said I was very suspicious. I said that's the way. She said it had their name and the date on the inside. John and Mary 1995. Only no and.

Fair enough, I said.

You're a good man, she said, to be trying so hard to find the person.

I showed her the ring. She had to get her reading glasses. She went into the kitchen to get them. You could see her knickers through the skinnies. I noticed that there was a wheelchair folded up. When she came back I asked her about it. My son, she said, he died, we're giving the chair back. I said I was sorry for her trouble.

She looked inside the ring. That's it, she said. She took off her diamond ring and then her wedding ring and showed me the inside. It was the match.

Fair enough, I said. Is there a reward?

She look at me. What reward?

I looked down. Then I looked up. I winked. I remember my dad winking. He was a ladies' man.

I saw her blushing.

It was just embarrassing. I looked away and I saw that there was a pair of work boots beside the wheelchair. They had steel toecaps.

Are you throwing the boots out too?

What are you talking about?

Are the boots going with the chair?

Oh no, she said, they're my husband's spares. He's in work.

Well, I said, that's nice isn't it. Not too much of that around here.

What are you after, she said. What kind of a reward?

I didn't look at her. I said, You were flogging your husband's ring at the We Buy Gold. I wonder why? Let's see what you have inside the pants so.

What the actual fuck, she said. Is this a joke?

As a reward Missus, I said. It's easy peasy.

She started to close the door. I put my foot in it but she got it closed anyway. It hurt bad. From inside she shouted at me. Get the fuck out of here you spa.

That wasn't nice. People called me that before. I don't put up with it.

Then I noticed that a neighbour she had was looking at me out the window. They don't like the neighbours talking. All my neighbours in 17 Girvan Buildings are students. I'm the last real person. You should see the goings-on.

Mary, I said. I knocked on the door. Mary are you in there? The neighbours are looking. You'll be a show.

I could hear her inside the door. I said, I'm going down the We Buy Gold with your ring.

Oh Jesus no, she said.

Oh Jesus yes, I said.

Wait, she said. I waited. After a few minutes she opened the door. I stepped in. She closed the door behind me.

Look, she said, you're a nice man. Just give me the ring please.

I shook my head. Can't. Have to have a reward like.

I'm going to do it, she said. You can look but no touching. Right?

I was happy. My dad would be proud. A ladies' man.

But you better give me the ring, she said, or I'll fucking slaughter you.

She was a lot smaller than me. They don't get enough to eat and they grow up small and stalky. But they're rough. You never know what they'll do. They're dirty fighters up on the hill. That's what my dad said.

Just get it off, I said, knickers and all.

I watched.

When she had it all down around her knees I got a good look at her. It was my first time apart from magazines. I was sorry I didn't have a camera but my phone is useless. A video would be nice. I was a bit disappointed frankly. But still it was all right.

That was nice, thanks very much, I said. Politeness costs nothing. I gave her the ring.

She stared at me. Is that all you want?

That was the deal, I said. Fair's fair.

She pulled up her knickers and her skinnies.

You're some weirdo. Are you a gay or something? A mammy's boy?

I hit her in the face. It's years since I hit anything. Since my dad was teaching me.

She fell down. She tripped on the boots. I'd say she was surprised.

She started to get up so I hit her again. I didn't hit her hard. Just a tap. You have to be able to control yourself, my dad used to say. You have to learn to pull your punches. She was crying and making noise. It was irritating. I don't like noise. Sometimes a woman has a kid in a pram and the kid is crying. I hate that. I go up to her and say, Missus will you stop the child crying? And usually they do. It's always the skanky ones. Sometimes they give you a piece of their mind.

You're just a skanky slut, I said. Shut up or I'll give you another one.

Give them something to remember my dad used to say.

I picked up the boots. I need these, I said.

She was gone quiet. She was feeling her nose which was bleeding. She had her T-shirt pulled up to stop the blood. It was all red now. It looked funny. I could see her bellybutton which was nice.

Then I saw the ring on the floor.

I picked it up and looked at it again. John•Mary•1995. I was thinking it was good that I found the Mary and she was willing. Even if she said no first I didn't hold it against her. I put it on the table. Fair is fair. I found it but I gave it back. Time to go and, as my dad used to say, no time like the present. I opened the door and there was a man standing outside. He had on a T-shirt that said Guns N' Roses. He was bald. Or at least shaved. He was smaller than me. He had a pair of work boots with steel toe-caps. Stay away from street fighters, my dad used to say.

Who are you? he said. And what the fuck are you doing with my boots?

Are you John of John and Mary 1995? I found your ring.

I saw him looking over my shoulder. Jesus, Mary, he said. What happened to you?

And Joseph, I giggled. I couldn't help it. Jesus, Mary and Joseph.

Then he looked back at me. I saw him shift his weight in his boots. I knew what he was doing.

STATEMENT REGARDING THE RECENT
HUMAN SOUL EXPERIMENTS

I have to say I was sworn to secrecy of course, my boss insisted on that. So that makes it, to say the least, difficult maybe even impossible for me to be totally honest about what happened, let alone how I felt about it, which was complicated. I have to say straight out that I was brought up a Catholic. Which is like even more complicated if anything. So to make a long story short, we found it easy enough once we knew what we were looking for. He didn't tell me of course. I'm only the technician and techies never hear the big picture. But he had the whole game-plan nailed to the last letter. I have to say I have massive admiration for the boss. The day of the final press-conference was a total blast for everybody, yours truly included. The media all expected a thing like an organ and there was research that looked at the brain, of course, using PET scans and all that other stuff but they were all wrong. He knew it all along that they were totally out.

The properties listed in Appendix B were identified by me completely, which he later claimed in the paper were his own discoveries, but I can authenticate my statements from laboratory notebooks and also private notebooks which, surprise surprise, coincide exactly with the laboratory ones. I have kept a private diary of the experiments since the boss first detailed to me exactly what it was he was wanting me to do. Which makes even more sense, going forward, seeing what he is claiming. I would like to say that I was never comfortable but he assured me: a. that it was completely legal and b. that there were no ethics problems, which is important to me because I have always valued my professional qualifications — although, to be honest, they never exactly spelled out what was ethical and what was not, I tended to stick fairly closely to what was legal.

As far as I'm concerned, the things in the media are way-off. We never used cadavers or anything like that; we didn't use aborted foetuses or any material derived from aborted foetuses or pre-born babies or whatever. All our subjects were alive before and after the experiments. Some of them twigged a bit what was going on I suppose, fair dues. We used adult males and females which was the best part for me to be honest. Let's face it, no male is ever going to hate wiring up a young healthy female no matter what shape she's in, generally speaking, and some of them of course were not the best. To be honest, the kind of people who sign up for these type of experiments are generally druggies or something, very rarely middle class college students, know what I mean? But they didn't have much in the way of morals I have to say anyway; they tended to not care very much about taking their clothes off and so on and getting wired up. Of course we weren't interested in having them freaking out or anything, so we tended to give them something nice to pass the time, you know the stuff they give you in these situations, like going for an operation they don't want you freaking out on the table when they all arrive in the green suits and masks, so they give you something nice to keep everything nice and cool you know, and this may well have been one of the reasons why they were, as the boss liked to put it, totally compliant, they couldn't get enough of that stuff actually as you can imagine. It is untrue that we gave them amnesiac drugs which anyway I had only heard of in media reports about rapes. And if you ask them, if you can find enough of them, they'll be able to testify that they remember it all, if they remember anything at all being mostly crackheads et cetera. With the money we paid them they could certainly get their hands on all that kind of thing. My guess is they're totally blasted. Fused, know what I mean?

I have to say, I paid them a little extra for services rendered, the ones that rendered services, which anyway they were fairly used to doing by way of getting the stuff they used. So it was nothing new to them or nothing special anyway. It cost me a fair whack out of the old wage packet because I used to go in every evening to see that they were nicely settled down for the night, they had all the best stuff in their rooms, DVD players and a coffee-maker and they could get quite sexy DVDs, which I sometimes watched with them and then sort of popped the question straight out because it was a business arrangement and I didn't want either of us to feel in any way embarrassed about it because we both knew where we stood. Sometimes they agreed and sometimes they did not; if they did not agree I did not press the matter further. Actually I managed it almost every night, I was making hay you know because I could see, going forward, that the experiment would not go on forever, but they were frequently quite horny anyway, hanging around naked in this gorgeous room perfectly heated and air conditioned and I often saw them at it themselves in an off and on kind of way; not wearing any clothes, they became sort of shameless and animal about it, they'd have the old hand down there even when you were talking to them sometimes, which was partly the drugs we were giving them.

To be honest, I kept a financial record of all those transactions which I have at home because I wanted everything to be above board. They appreciated the money too and there was no harm done. So, as far as I'm concerned, I'm prepared to be completely open about that, that's no secret, the papers have that bang-on and it's no reflection on my boss who didn't know about it; we didn't have any kind of surveillance because the experiment didn't require it and it would have been fairly undignified for all these people to be living and sleeping in rooms with cameras following them everywhere. The funny thing is we have cameras everywhere else except in the subject rooms.

So that is how I could record the response to stimuli. And I can give you an exclusive on this; there is a proportional relationship between the strength of the energy field and the amount of pleasure, and, surprise surprise, it is not an inverse, which is totally not what all the churches have been saying which, going forward, is going to lead to a total reassessment of some of the traditional commandments.

Most people expect the soul to be a. an organ (the simple view) or b. a complete myth (also now a simple view we proved). The fact is the soul is exactly as described. The boss's paper has it nailed and that's the best place to get the exact details and definitions and so on, I'm more concerned here with the allegations and my own reputation. And the worst allegation, as far as I'm concerned, is far and away the one about me and the men. I would like to say I did not have sexual relations with the men. I hold my hands up about the women, no problem, been there done that, but I am not gay. Those allegations are false and without foundation and the man who made them was well sorted by the media, who bought him off, no doubt about it to be honest. I have to say I was the victim of a vicious and unprovoked assault by that particular gentleman which I recorded in the laboratory log and I had to defend myself, which I was an amateur boxer in my teens and I know how to handle my fists and that is the reason that we had that fight which I hold my hands up about. That certainly happened and I think my side of the story can be believed easily enough when you remember that the subject had a medical record that included mild schizophrenia. I wouldn't be here breaking confidentiality if he didn't make uncalled-for allegations in the media. I would like to state I have total self-control and would never lose the rag over that kind of provocation.

The last fact that I would like to express is to bury the allegation that we stole the subjects' souls. This allegation is a laugh. If you read the boss' paper, you will see that the soul is not a concrete thing and the energy on which it lives is intricately linked to the biological entity, as he says himself, in other words souls are personal. They can't be just lifted. We are not at that stage of development. I have to say one thing though and that is, we did observe a small incidence of not being able to locate souls in certain subjects after a given time, which was totally random and like crap from the procedure point of view. We were always having to re-calibrate our systems and double-check our measurements for everyone. We worked it out that the levels fluctuated on some unknown principle, I quote the boss, it appears as though the subjects could have more or less soul, which I like the way he put it. Because I did not reveal my nocturnal activities, I was unable to inform him that I knew several of the affected subjects fairly well and that three of the girls in particular were the most compliant and had been very good to me and also had the lowest levels. I am preparing a paper on this idea myself so I'll say no more about it for now but I will go further in the relevant professional journals. To be honest, these same subjects which I refer to, came out of the whole thing well-up on their fees on account of my extra-contractual payments. I know for a fact one of them went straight and now owns a half share in a dry-cleaning business which is doing well. I take my kit there so I should know.

The boss is always talking the big picture but I'm only a techie so I keep my eye on the ball and I have to say in this instance, that it was a pleasure to be involved in proving at least one thing about religion right. I'm proud to have been involved in an experiment that established beyond doubt the existence of the human soul, it worked out well all round, apart from the few complainants, who anyway would have been complaining no matter what.

The boss has already outlined the positive benefits, such as religion being able to use our system to assess souls instead of confessions and stuff, and the possible applications, going forward, for alternative therapies and the cosmetics industry. But one thing he avoided, which I have to say is at the entirely experimental stage, is if it's possible to remove or even diminish a subject's soul then a. it could be used to punish criminals b. it could be used as a means of controlling children on the reward system and c. it should be possible, going forward, to buy and sell souls or possibly even total soul replacement.

I am involved with patenting a process, that is totally at the experimental stage, that can identify people who are more susceptible to diminished soul, which is not covered by the boss's patents or copyrights. A totally new system that has incredible potential for the Church, the police, the government and private enterprise. Which, being a Catholic myself, is like totally exciting for me. Thank you.

I FOLLOW A CHARACTER

I see Jo Strane in the market. She is buying fish. At first I am shocked by how much older she looks, then I calculate that about twenty years has elapsed, maybe more. Chronology was always my worst point. I would work away confident that the chronology would fall into place, or could be corrected later, and then my editor would come back with a table of errors proving that none of the people could be as old at such and such a time, or that a certain child would be four or forty by the time such and such an event occurred.

She is thin. Her hair is streaked grey in places and not very full. She looks like she has been using the wrong shampoo for twenty years. She buys a single fillet of plaice so I conclude she lives alone. I am not surprised. I follow her at a discreet distance and watch her buy new potatoes from the man with the big hands and the arthritic knuckles. He tells her the usual, that the potatoes are from Ballycotton and that he has good spinach. As always he looks away when he is talking to her; I have the impression that he is looking directly at me, but I know it's a habit he has developed over the years, a form of politeness perhaps. She goes out onto Prince's Street then and turns left. She has that same wary walk. She goes into Porter's and buys a newspaper—I can't see which one. She asks for a bag and while the girl is fishing under the counter for it, Jo lifts a magazine off the shelf and slips it into her coat. She pays for the bag and the newspaper and leaves.

Later at the bus-stop I see that the magazine is called *Kitchens*.

It used to be *Homes & Gardens*. I can only speculate about the intervening action. Was she arrested for the murder of little Robin? Did she go on to destroy another life? Did she, at some point, either through psychotherapy or force of will, come to a full or partial understanding of what she had done, such an understanding as I had deliberately chosen not to give her? Did she, during that time of anguish, form a concept of me? Or, to paraphrase Aquinas, did she conceive of what I am not but fail in what I am? Aquinas was writing about God, and I am conscious of falling into the familiar false trope of the writer as omnipotent deity. Nevertheless, even God must be constrained by the forces he devised, otherwise miracles would be commonplaces.

I notice that her breasts have never developed. This was something that escaped me before. I think it fits—arrested development. She probably suffers from amenorrhea too. Had I noticed this or did she have periods at the time? I think that perhaps I should return to my original notebooks. She wears shoes that are part-way between trainers and proper shoes. The light coat is not out of place on a dull, cool June day in Ireland, but underneath she wears something like a party-frock, a confection of green silky material with sequins in the bodice and a flared a-line skirt. I suspect that she bought it, second-hand, at the Conquer Cancer shop, or Oxfam.

I decide to risk standing in the same bus-shelter. I slip into the far corner and at first pretend to read a poster that advertises the dangers of smoking. Then I turn round and looked directly at her. She glances at me but does not appear to recognise me.

My first reaction is disappointment. Then I think about the impossibility of any contact between creator and created. It would be like the simultaneous arrival in a particular spot of anti-matter and matter. The collision would erase the space in which it occurred. Nothingness would remain. Perhaps she can't see me at all, or whatever lapse in the fabric of things presents her to me is a one-way glass, a non-reflexive function; or perhaps she sees me only in whatever terms she originally conceived of me in, as an indifferent stranger perhaps, someone who didn't really matter to her, or who didn't understand her.

Then I think about Simone Weil's dictum that we must prefer a real hell to an imaginary paradise. Jo Strane has not failed to recognise me but rather at some profound level refused to conceive of my existence. She has chosen to be in her own real hell rather than believe that there exists a creature who could re-write the whole story, or revise the ending or the beginning as an American publisher asked me to do, or devise a new second story in which she might be saved from herself. Or one who could have given her a different existence. I recall how, when I was a teenager crippled by Still's Disease, I raged against the God that I then believed in for choosing me to inflict himself on. How quickly I arrived at the Cathar's complaint, that God must also have created and foreseen the existence of evil and was therefore not a loving bystander in the Fall, expulsion and subsequent curse of knowledge and suffering, but the one who conceived and executed the whole sadistic mess. My response, the only rational one in the circumstances, was to become an atheist.

I try to imagine what pain has brought her to this point and I know that the time is not long enough and that I am not equipped. I chose, several years ago, to write a full stop to her life, knowing full well that there are no full stops in reality. That dot signified my own failure of attention, a refusal to remain engaged, a willingness to sacrifice the contingency of truth in favour of shape and form and a clever ending. I had relinquished her, and over the intervening years experienced at different paces in our different universes (four or five in mine, twenty or more in hers) she had come to certain conclusions about me, not the least of which was that I wasn't worth believing in.

She takes the Number Eleven and I follow. In the bus she sits very still, never turning her head. She doesn't seem to notice external things, this charming shabby city where I live, its people with their hearts of gold, silver and lead. I follow her when she gets out. I see her fiddle for her keys. The magazine is now in the bag with the newspaper. Up here, high on the hill the wind is stronger and the bag blows about uncertainly. Before she can put the key in the lock the door opens and a child of six or seven stands there. She steps through the door and turns with her hand on the latch. At this moment she looks straight at me. Then the door closes. Afterwards there is no sign of movement, no lights coming on — it is now early evening — no noise.

I may be a little in love with her. I recall doing something very similar once, many years ago, when I was at college — following a girl to her flat and watching the lights going on, hoping she wouldn't look out.

PERFECTION COMES TOO LATE

I keep getting this email. It may be something I have signed up for, but I suspect not. Sometimes it comes with a return address that turns out to be fake. Here is the text:

> Even if you have no erectin problems SOFT CIAzLIS would help you to make BETTER SE X MORE OFTEN! and to bring unimagnable plesure to her. Just disolve half a pil under your tongue and get ready for action in 15 minutes. The tests showed that the majority of men after taking this medic ation were able to have PERFECT ER ECTI ON during 36 hours!

Who is sending me this message? How do they know where I am? It worries me. Another aspect that worries me is the way certain words are broken. ER ECTI ON. So far as I know, these words, with the exception of the last, exist independently in no living language. They may be a code, or they may be typos. Simple, to dissolve a pill under the tongue (I'm translating here), and bring unimaginable pleasure to her, fifteen minutes to action, and it has been tested on the majority of men, which is reassuring.

The thing is, I have not clicked on the link provided.

Partly because I'm not sure what I'd do with a thirty-six hour erection.

Also because I'm always so uncertain as to the outcome. Some men approach women from a position of certainty. There is some arcane sign, some feral perfume that tells them that the object of their actions is ready to capitulate. Whereas I have never been in a position to be certain, even during coitus, that the woman I was with was having a good time. This is linked to persistent self-doubts that have troubled me ever since I was an adolescent; however, I detest those writers who, at the first opportunity, work back into a comfortable childhood setting, and blame, usually, their parents, or their upbringing (Catholic, for example), or some central figure in their past like a priest, for what, let's face it, is an adult failing. Children are supposed to be uncertain, but as adults they should learn to be happy.

Happy men certainly are more attractive to women. If I were a radio-talk show psychologist this is the first principle I would lay down. Be happy and secure and you will pull women. Whereas what radio-talk shows usually say is something like, Learn to love yourself. Which used to be called onanism.

Er ecti on sounds like the beginning of an alphabet though. *Alpha beta kappa, er, ecti, on.* I sometimes think that an alphabet exists in which my strange state of existence is perfectly described. Given that we shape reality through language, perhaps even create it, perhaps there should be a personalized alphabet for everybody. I'm surprised that a guru hasn't worked this one out.

So the email arrived again. My wife heard the ping while I was in the bathroom, and since we were expecting news from our daughter in Australia (a boy, seven pounds one ounce, Mark William) she read it. The title gave nothing away, it was just a random piece of text that happened to contain the word babble.

So, she said, why have you been making these enquiries?

It's just spam, I said, I get spam all the time.

Then I made a mistake. I said, They're idiots.

My wife assumed that this addition implied some kind of personal relationship. It's a reasonable reading of the expression.

So, she said, have you bought other stuff from them? How did they get you on their list?

Everyone is on their list, I said.

She folded her arms and looked at me. My wife is an American. This is a classic American gesture that I first saw on the Jack Benny Show. Jack Benny always accompanied the gesture with a slight turn of his head and the words, Do you believe this? Something like that anyway.

So after that she found my MSN records. I've been saving them in order to fine-tune my responses, although, as it happens, I haven't gotten around to actually re-reading them. I don't think she read them in full either. MSN records are virtually unreadable. LOL and NBD and all that stuff. It took me a long time to learn the code, fortunately I found a useful site with an alphabeticised list that went something like this:

Acronym	Meaning
AFAIK	As far as I know
AIM	AOL Instant Messenger
ASL	Age/Sex/Location
ATM	At the moment
BRB	Be right back

Most of which I never came across anyway. I never met anyone online who really used it. And there were smileys for everything anyway. It's probably true that if there's an alphabeticised list nobody uses it anymore and in fact one girl told me that using things like that meant I was a beginner.

So she said to me, Who are these people? What does R U OK mean?

It means Are You OK.

Is this you asking this girl are you OK?

That's me. Or at least that's the me on MSN.

What the hell are you talking about? she said.

What you're reading.

So, she said, Are you OK implies that whatever came before this was something that might upset her. She says What? then you type R U OK and then you type this ::[]:: What is that? Where is the question you asked her? It's not in this file.

I don't know.

What does that symbol mean?

It's a Band-Aid.

What?

It's what they call an emoticon. It means I'm offering support.

You're offering this girl support?

Assuming she is a girl.

My wife walked out of the room. Then she walked back in again. What is going on? she said.

I said, Sit down, you're making me nervous.

So, my wife said, you pretended to be a psychologist.

I do have some experience...

Oh yes, thanks to me.

She looked at me a little longer. Her father, Jeff, was an engineer who worked on hydro-electric projects. He was a tall man with a slight stoop. He served in the Navy during the war. He didn't talk about it. Her mother was a doctor who never practised. When they visit us they exude a kind of generosity and warmth that after a few days is overwhelming and makes me want to hit one of them.

And what has happened?

Nothing. They tell me their stories. Or the stories they want to tell me. And I console them.

She laughed. You console them?

Yes. I'm an older wiser man who has seen a lot of life.

She laughed again.

And I give them words of wisdom.

Now she stared at me intensely. So, what did you say to this girl here? Level with me now.

I told her she should sleep with her boyfriend.

What?

I said chances like that may not come twice.

For a long while my wife said nothing. She looked at me and looked away several times. She folded her arms and unfolded them.

I said, You'd need to know her. Things are bad for her.

My wife got up and went to the kitchen sink. She ran the cold tap and stood watching the flow for a few moments with her hand still on the lever. It's a stainless steel lever, a Franke, and Jeff wanted to take the tap apart last time he was over—to see how the valve worked. The stream comes out milky-looking because of some filter in the pipe. It's milky because it's full of turbulence and air bubbles.

You think five or six sessions with a shrink makes you an expert?

I said I didn't think there was a lot to it. I said I thought most psychologists were paid to dispense common sense and it was only the fact that they were paid that gave it any authority.

Level with me, do you want to fuck these girls?

I don't even know that they are girls. This is the internet. They could be fifty year old married men.

Have you ever met any of them?

I looked at my wife. One thing I would like to have done at that moment was change the balance of power. I thought about what would happen if I said yes. I imagined describing the meeting, the girl, what we said, how I seduced her, her eagerness. But I also thought my wife would immediately recognise it as some kind of weak fantasy.

No.

Would you like to?

No.

So you get your kicks out of this remote control relationship where you're the wise old owl and she's the frail adolescent. Didn't you get enough of frail adolescence with Maya? Remember when she went to that disco and she came home in bits. You passed her on to me like a hot coal. You didn't want to console her. You wanted to get rid of her. You went into the den and turned on the TV while she was crying. And when I asked you to visit with his parents you said you couldn't face it. I had to do it myself. Imagine how that made me feel, a woman, going about a thing like that? At least they were nice about it. At least they took Maya's side.

I remember.

Well what is it? What's driving you to this? Are you worried about money? I saw you watching that stuff about the banks on television? Are you worried about your pension? Is it fear driving you?

I'm not being driven. I just like doing it that's all. I'm their agony-aunt.

Is it me?

Aw fuck, I said, it's always you.

Ever since you had that little problem, she said.

My wife is still beautiful. She was beautiful in that American way when I met her and she still is. She buys her clothes from the Sears & Roebuck catalogue. She wears Classic Elements Pull-on Twill Pants and Covington Twill. She wears an Apostrophe Three Quarters Sleeve Sateen

Blouse. I know because it is one of our rituals, browsing through the S&R catalogue and choosing that season's look, which has turned out to be, over twenty-seven or so seasons, the same look every year. It's a kind of beauty that wears thin. She has perfect teeth and wears her hair short. She took creative writing at Colombia and, when I met her, used to describe herself as an author.

I told one of the girls that I specialised in adolescent psychology. I said I hoped she didn't mind being called an adolescent. She said she couldn't even spell it. I also said I had medical training, which is true. I told another that I wrote a syndicated agony-aunt column for newspapers in the United States. Do they syndicate agony-aunts? She asked me if I just made up the answers. I was touched by the simplicity of the question.

After she found my MSN records, my wife tried to get me to make love to her. She thought if she used what she called my fantasy thoughts about these girls...

I said, Look, I like helping them. I think I can make their lives better. I like them telling me their stories. It helps them.

She said, You should go back to the doctor.

I said, I don't have any problems to talk to him about. I'm a happy man.

So while I was away at a conference I checked out the link. It looked shabby like a scam, a bit garish, tacky, some of the buttons didn't work — which is exactly what I expected, but even so I felt cheated. I was away from home and I was ready for something. I didn't know what. Who buys drugs on the internet anyway? Who would be that crazy? So instead I had a few at the hotel bar and tried to initiate a conversation with a woman who had a laptop beside her. I told her about the email and we laughed over it together. I was implying that thirty six hours of sex was not beyond the bounds of possibility. She was at the same conference and had similar interests. She was thin and tall. She had intense blue eyes. After about an hour I became terrified of their blueness. She had unbuttoned her jacket and was complaining that she had eaten too much and that her slacks were too tight. She loosened her belt even. We were talking about young people and saying that one of the great joys of our profession was being able to help them. Then we were joined by other people. It turned out she and I were the only people not worried about pensions. There was a general feeling of desperation. Then someone mentioned a club that ran in the basement at the back of the hotel. You had to walk out onto the street and around the corner. Everyone at the conference had a free pass, they said. It was in our conference folder. I said I would follow them over. But instead, when I got to my room, I powered up the laptop and took another look at that site. I wondered if having a thirty six hour erection would be empowering. It could easily be painful. I ordered some anyway, and paid by credit card. I had them send it to my home address and I put my wife's name on it and asked them to gift-wrap the package.

LOL, I would have written if I were on MSN.

I'm laughing out loud.

I am in fact an orthodontist. I used to be a dentist but after a couple of years extracting and filling teeth, cleaning teeth and prescribing things for gingivitis and so on, dentistry becomes a little like a kind of antique restoration. Orthodontics offer some opportunity for artistic expression. I believe the mouth is the focal organ for the entire personality. Orthodontic manipulation has all of the characteristics of drama: the longed-for perfection, the purgative suffering, the adjustment, the epiphany, catharsis. There was once this beautiful girl with a terrible mouth who came to me; overcrowding was turning her into a kind of large-beaked bird. I extracted some teeth and set up a brace system. I'm going to put a beautiful smile in your face, I told her. I fitted Hawley retainers. I didn't say that teeth move throughout life; that if she wanted everything to stay the way it should be she would have to wear retainers every day from then on. By the time she was twenty I was finished the reconstructive phase. Then she didn't turn up and I found out she died. I see in those steel wires a metaphor for inexorable time. Perfection comes too late as always.

EVERY DAMN STAR THAT SHINES

When I cried out there in the water it was just a sudden rush, something broke, it wasn't anything I was thinking about before. It was a surprise. A shock in fact. I walked out into the sea as far as my waist and then I just stood there as if I didn't know what to do. In that instant I really didn't know. Then I noticed that I was crying and making noise. I think it was the temperature of the water, strange as that may sound. It was cold. The sea here is drop-dead beautiful and I swim a lot but it gets deep maybe ten feet from the shore. You stand at the edge and you take a step forward and then it's nearly ten feet down. The charts show that it is, as they say, profound, and because of the shape of the bay most of the fish and plankton of this closed sea wash in here at some time. It's warm and rich in summer, but at this time of the year the depth makes it very cold. It shines in the morning and in the evening and sometimes when the moon rises it shines then too. The moon shines in our window. Bob likes to sit and look at it in the dark sometimes. But he reads on a Kindle so it doesn't matter so much to him. I need light, light, light. God, I need the sun and the moon and every damn star that shines. Bob was standing there on the beach when I broke. I didn't have to look around because I knew it. He was standing there in his rust-red Slam bathing costume watching me with those knowing eyes of his. He knew. He knew what was happening and he didn't come out to get me. That's part of his wisdom. He could have come out but he never does. You're a swimmer, he always says, I just flop around on the edge of happening. He says I go too far. I swim out beyond the buoys that stop the yachts from coming in. Bob grew up in New York. I was the water to his rock. When I came in from Vancouver he was there. I met him in my first lecture. It was like he was always there waiting for me to come in, or I was always journeying towards that spot where he stood.

When I started to cry I wasn't aware at first. That was a strange thing. I thought I was just looking at the sea. In fact I didn't think at all, I was just looking. Then I became aware of the noise I was making and that people in the water—two old French men who swim every day, and a younger woman who swims at weekends—were looking at me strangely. In fact they were alarmed. The French woman swam a steady breaststroke in my direction. Her eyes watched me steadily. Her hair was wet. It looked like a smooth black helmet that reached to her shoulders and trailed in the water. She didn't say a word. I heard the two men talking. They were swimming too. They always swam together. I suspect they were talking about me. They were straining their necks to keep their faces dry. Like dogs keeping their heads up. I could hear their breathing coming towards me. And then I heard my own voice. It was coming from low down somewhere that I didn't know was there. What does it mean? These things are signs, always signs. What does it signify?

What I do is I launch myself head down in the water. Underwater I make no sound. I hold the sound inside though I feel it moving in me like a wave. I swim underwater for as long as possible. I keep my eyes open. I see the bright dead ocean floor of the Mediterranean drifting by, and then I'm out onto the glassy deep where nothing happens. If this was a different sea I would hear whale sounds and they would be the exact equivalent of the sound-wave in my body. The great whales calling to each other. I figure, that's what I am. But who am I calling for?

Bob knows, of course.

When I surface he's there. He knows I'm going to surface. He never fears for me. He's watching me. He's taken his sunglasses off. He waves that uncertain wave of his. He's not uncertain at all but it's the way he waves. He mouths the words, Everything ok? I nod my head. I'm ok. We're not two Americans going to make spectacles of ourselves on a French beach in wintertime. I put my head down and stroke away, out deep. It's only March and there are no boats to worry about. I swim right out into the *rade*. Out there I can see as far as the Upper Corniche Road. I can see the last snow on the high peaks. We saw snow fall on these narrows, falling on the beach and whitening above the waterline, falling in the olive groves and the roofs, whitening the red tiles. It was so beautiful it would break your heart. It fell for a night and a day and the people here said they had never seen such a snowfall in their lifetimes. They all came out to see it. They closed the school and the shops on the middle and high roads. People were excited. So were we. Bob and I have seen plenty of snow, but the place makes all the difference. That's something I've worked out about snow. And maybe a lot of other things. Places make things happen.

But when I started to walk back I couldn't do it. I felt naked. I know tears make everyone feel that way, but I was ashamed of the noise. Maybe if I understood it I might be able to bear it, but I didn't. It just came out of me. First I was swimming. Then I stopped in about five feet something. It was up to my chest. I couldn't go any further. I was afraid it would start again. Waves don't move, things circulate inside the wave, but the wave never moves on. Think of a rope. When you flick it a wave travels along it, but the rope stays in the same place. The tension and the twist remain the same, it's the same rope always. This is the substance of what I spent my life studying — waves and particles and what we laughingly call fluid dynamics. Not anymore.

Of course I came all the way out of the water in the end. It was too cold to stay there except as some kind of petrified figure from mythology. I don't qualify. And Bob was waiting with the towel. We didn't speak. I stepped out of the water and turned and stepped backward into his arms and he enclosed me in the rough dry warmth of the towel. That's the way it's always been. My pirouette, his embrace. We get along.

We sat on the sand. It's more fine gravel here, or at least a very coarse sand. It felt good. The sun felt good.

Bob, I said, I want to say it feels good to be alive but more than that. I want to say it's good be alive with you.

He laughed but he knew.

Do you remember that Godard film we saw a few weeks ago? *Le Petit Soldat?*

Yes, I do.

You know there's a moment when he's being tortured, though they're not torturing him at that exact time, but he's in the bathroom chained to that damned thing on the wall, and he just looks straight at the camera. Do you remember that?

Yes, I do.

Well, his face looks completely different to any other shot in the film. I was thinking about that as we walked down here and I realized it may be the only time he looks at the camera in the entire film. He's always looking down or at someone else. I believe that's a very important shot. I can't work out what it's saying. I realize now I don't understand that film at all. Out there on the water I saw his face.

It's because he reminds you of Harry.

I looked at him. How did he know that? I was never going to tell him.

It's because of what he went through, he said.

We gathered our things. The French men were sitting on the sand with their backs to the sea-wall. The woman was towelling herself. She looked fit and well. I wondered if she lived here all year round. Something told me she came from somewhere else.

Bob, do you remember when we went to see Susan that time? The last time, before we came over here?

He nodded. I thought she was holding it together well. The kids were great.

You were in the TV room watching the game and I offered to help with the cooking. Remember? Well, we got talking and I saw that she was getting angry and I didn't want the kids to hear, so I closed the kitchen door. Harry's old jacket was hanging on the back.

His hunting jacket?

We both laughed. Harry never hunted but every couple of years he invested in the latest Columbia Sportswear camouflage jacket. He liked walking. I used to say, What are you hiding from, Harry? You don't want camouflage, you want to be seen, someone is going to shoot you someday by mistake.

So his jacket was there, he said. She forgot to throw it out. Or maybe she couldn't bear to.

No, I said, she forgot it.

The sun was beginning to drop behind the town. It sets early here because of the height to the west, and then it gets cold. We walked up there once in the early days, an hour's walk, and stood at the old fort on the hill watching the darkness moving on the sea from Capt Ferrat to Cap D'Antibes. That evening for the first time I said to Bob something I've often said since: Bob, do you realize where we are? And he replied, We're doing the grand tour two hundred years too late. And we both laughed. I grew up on a logger's float-house on the Strait of Georgia. My dad was a logger until I was nine and then he had his accident. Harry and I used to collect clams and keep them in a galvanized tub and feed them on oatmeal until they got fat. I never eat clams now.

She got so angry, I said. She was shouting at the hunting jacket. I said to her, Susan you have to let go, and she said, I never close that damn door. I just never saw it. Bob, you should have seen the look on her face.

Bob said nothing.

Well, she took that coat down fast. She went out back and put it straight into the garbage. That was the worst moment. I watched her open the can and get it right in there. There was something violent, you know? Something hard.

Suddenly Bob was angry. He stopped walking. He was trudging

through the sand with his head down. Now he took his sunglasses off and turned full on to me.

What do you expect, Ali? For Christ's sake he could have done something. We all have to face it. He could have saved himself, that's the thing. That's what gets Susan angry. He didn't even try.

He looked at me for a while. I couldn't think of anything to say. Then he put those damn shades on and we walked up the sand and onto the sidewalk. We didn't say anything. I was trying to cope with what was inside. It felt like an animal had slipped in out of the dark.

Do you think we could move here, Bob?

He shook his head. Maybe before the crash. Not now.

His pension was down big-time. His college put it in some kind of fund that went with Bear Sterns or about that time. We stopped following it. Harry's business went the same road. We all know about derivatives now.

What I keep thinking about is this: What went through his head at the last minute. I can see his face as clear as if he was here this minute. I can see his eyes.

Don't think about it.

But Bob, he never owned a gun. He couldn't even hunt with dad.

Jesus, Ali. Stop.

It comes back. All the time.

Bob shook his head. Who knows? It's impossible to know.

Maybe we shouldn't have come down here, Bob. We blew a lot of money on this.

As we turned to climb the steps that brought us up to Rue Du Poilu where our room was, I said, Bob I'm frightened.

He took my hand and held it tightly.

The street was dark already. The light was on in the butcher shop ahead. I was cold. I pressed close to him. In that moment, for no good reason, and though he was not a swimmer, I felt he would save me, should the need ever arise.

TELLING

In the high cold room there were sixteen boys. Each boy had the space for one bed and a bedside locker. Under each bed was a suitcase containing clothes, comics, football boots. In there went wet gear after games because it was forbidden to hang wet clothes on the bed for health reasons. Generally there was nothing in the bedside locker. Nobody had a watch or a clock because all time was marked by bells. At half past six, for example a bell rang. Between then and the next bell at quarter to seven the boys were expected to wash and dress. At quarter to seven they were to move out of the dormitory towards the chapel. At seven o'clock the Mass bell rang. During Mass a little altar bell rang to inform them of the necessity to stand, sit or kneel. After Mass they were released for ten or fifteen minutes. Then at eight o'clock the refectory bell rang and they went in to breakfast. Breakfast was lumpy porridge and sometimes bread. A bell informed them that Father Tunny would say grace. They all stood, repeated the prayer and its following injunctions and sat down again. At that point, although no bell rang, they had permission to eat. Tunny was a bastard and everybody hated him. Sometimes he added a decade of the rosary to the grace so the porridge was stony cold when they sat down. The tea also was cooling.

Tunny was the Dean of Discipline.

He was the only teacher they had no nickname for. Others were Cocky, Snit, Weasel, Mucker. He was always just Tunny. Once a first year had gone to the staffroom and asked for Father Mucker. There had been laughing. Perhaps the priests and teachers knew their nicknames though they were supposed to be almost a secret code. But you could go to the staffroom and ask for Father Tunny and there would be no laughing.

First class on a Monday morning was maths with Tunny. It spoiled the weekend.

Tunny says, Come up to me, Billy boy.

You go up and he hands you the chalk. He wants you to prove the theorem. So you start to draw the triangle or the line or whatever it is you have to draw. You start to write down the letters, a, b, c, or A, B, C. Capitals and smalls are important. You have to get them right. You know if you get them wrong because you hear Tunny snickering behind your back. You rub them out and change them, small for capital or vice versa. Then you start to put up the writing. If you get the first line wrong. That's when you know you're alive.

Tunny says, Turn round.

You turn round.

Hold out your hand.

You hold out your hand. He has a cane in a special pocket of his soutane. He holds your hand in a special way, with his thumb crooked over your thumb. He has soft fat hands. Your father would say he had never done a day's work in his life, hands like that. Whing the cane comes down. It is a special cutting pain, not like a punch or a slap or like getting hit with a stick or a ruler. The pain is a straight line across your palm from a to b. If he gets angry it comes across your wrist which is too much altogether and will make you cry or even scream. Don't make him angry. You get one on each hand.

Now can you do it?

Or

That might help you concentrate.

So you turn back to the blackboard. But now all you can think about is getting the line wrong again or getting the next line wrong and that whing and the pain. What you don't understand is that this is a commonplace. All over the world people are getting it in the neck for fucking up the first line of Pythagoras. It is how the system works and it's for your own good.

Father Tunny prowls the dormitories at night. Sometimes he slips inside in the dark and waits at the door. After the bell for lights out there is meant to be silence. No talking between the beds. And no getting out of bed. If he's there and all. In the dark. You can't see the crows in the dark because of the black soutane. I think there's someone there. Sssh. Sixteen boys listen. I think he's there. The light comes on.

Tunny says, He is there. Who was talking?

Nobody owns up. If you own up you will be caned.

If the boy who was talking does not admit it everyone will be caned.

That is the way Tunny talks. He has grammar. Nobody owns up.

Right, everybody out.

You all get out and stand beside the bed. Tunny comes to the first bed. Right, he says, bend over.

The boy bends over and Tunny pushes him down on the bed. He grabs the string of his pyjamas and pulls it down. We all see his bare bottom. We are embarrassed. Boys do not like other boys to see their bottoms. Whing, whing, whing, whing. Four across the bum. We can see stripes. Then another four. Eight laces. Oh Jesus. The boy is crying. I didn't do it, I wasn't talking.

Tell me who was talking after lights out?

I don't know, I swear I don't know.

Do not swear child, God does not want you swearing.

Whing, whing, whing. Whing.

Twelve.

Next boy.

Oh Jesus, Mary and Joseph.

The next boy is crying already. He bends. Tunny pulls his pants down. Four quick ones. The same thing. Tell me. I don't know. Four more. Tell me now. Please Father, I don't know.

Twelve again.

Next boy.

Next boy.

The same for each boy except the cane is getting harder. The stripes are like lines in a diagram. Intersecting lines, radiating. How to prove the theorem. Twelve lines is too much. Nobody knows the theorem for twelve lines.

You're next. He knows your name. He laced you that very morning for Pythagoras.

Billy boy, he says. He smiles when he says it. Come here to me, Billy boy.

You don't know if you can stick it. You know who was talking. You take your twelve. After each four the pain is unbearable. That's why he stops to ask you. He wants you to feel it and know there's four more coming. You feel the pain in your hole and in your bollox and round in your belly. He's hitting low so he's coming close to the bollox all the time. Fuck the fucker, fuck the fucker. You say it in your head over and over again. Hoping you don't say it out loud.

Twelve of the best.

Next.

Nobody squeals. He cuts the second last boy. He draws blood. That's not supposed to happen. Each of us thinks if there was only someone we could tell. There is no one we can tell. It's not so much a secret as a thing that never happened. Nobody would believe it.

It's a song, Where have you been, Billy boy, Billy boy?

It's just mocking. If he was another boy you'd fight him for that.

If he keeps it up you'll kill him. In the dark you can cry. Sixteen boys crying without a sound. In the dark you can plan ways of killing him.

You try to think of the worst ways to kill him, but none of them is as bad as what he's doing because they come to an end and school is forever.

Come up to my room after ref, Billy boy, he said. So at ref you couldn't eat a thing. You went into his room. There was a smell of polish. There was a fire burning in the grate. There was a comfortable chair. There was a desk and another chair. The Dean's room was in the same part of the building where the boys' dormitories were because he was the Dean of Discipline. The other priests lived in a different part through a big wooden door with Private written over it. Also in Irish *Príobháideach*.

Tunny was sitting in the armchair.

Come here to me, Billy boy, he said.

You were to stand in front of him. He pointed at the spot on the carpet. You went and you stood where he said. He likes you, someone said. If he likes me. You don't know what's happening, standing there on the spot on the carpet. You start to cry.

Don't cry, Billy boy, he says, I'm not going to hurt you.

And when you went home for Christmas your mother said, How are you getting on with your cousin Father Tunny?

He's not my cousin, you said.

You said it without thinking but then you knew it was true. Of course he was your cousin.

It was a boarding school. How else could they afford it? Now you remembered seeing him before. In your own house. He pinched your cheek one time. A long time ago.

I was always one of his favourites, your mother said, smiling like a baby. When I was a little girl.

And that was the end of something too. Not innocence, of course, because childhood is a myth. Not childhood either. And it was not the end of love. But something ended that day and nothing has ever taken its place.

You twisted your ankle, turning suddenly to catch the ball. They sent you to the infirmary and the sister gave you aspirin and a cold compress. So you were sitting on a chair there with your foot on another chair and she was talking about the big strong men that were there when she was a girl and how they could lift this much or that much and how they used to challenge each other outside the blacksmith forge and the blacksmith could lift the anvil and no one else could. How old was she anyway? In those days you thought she was a hundred or more and maybe she was. She was a little wizened woman with a twist in her spine. People said she couldn't lie down in a bed because of that twist. And then other people said that nuns never lay down in bed anyway because of the temptation. They had to sleep with their hands outside the blankets. But she kept putting cold compresses on your ankle and chattering like she never met people and you were quite happy for once, for one day in that place. And then there was a tap on the door and Tunny came in.

How's the patient, Sister Michael?

Oh he'll live, Father, Sister Michael said. Turned his ankle is all.

Will he be off games?

He will.

Well now, he said, I'll give him a note. We'll give him tomorrow off classes too.

Sister Michael beamed. Lucky boy, she said. Then she got up and went into the other room. And your gut twisted in the sack of your belly. Like an animal inside. You could think of nothing but fear blinded and deafened you.

He sat down where Sister Michael had been sitting.

How are we, Billy, he said.

All right, Father.

That's my boy, he said.

He turned the compress. You should write a letter home, he said. How long is it now since you wrote to your poor mother? She must be thinking of you. I'll go and get pen and paper and you can write it while you're sitting here. It's better to have something to do.

All right, Father.

He came back in ten minutes with a letter pad, a pen and an envelope. He had a book too. It was *The Call of The Wild*. You read it afterwards. It was brilliant. He gave it into your hand. He didn't touch you. Then he took a bar of chocolate from his soutane and put it down beside your hand on the quilt.

He never said a word.

He looked around. The door to Sister Michael's dispensary room was closed. That was where she kept her pills. There were boys who were always talking about breaking in because there was good stuff in there. They never did.

He stood up. He kissed you softly on the forehead. Then he went out.

If ever you told anyone they would not have believed you. But you knew from the beginning that there was no telling.

THE CLEARING

The laurels are tongues lapping his face. Underfoot is dry hard ground and ferns. Shadows spill into his eyes. There is a path taking him up through the trees. Behind him he hears their voices, dry, hard, jeering.

Tommy? Come out now, Tommy.

We only want to talk to you, Tommy.

Tom-mie — mocking his mother.

His breathing is almost as loud. He can hear his feet on the drum ground. He cannot lift his legs fast enough. Ahead of him he sees the clearing. He can see streamers of light through the trees. Not laurel here but ash and sycamore. He thinks he hears whispering.

Suddenly he bursts into the open and feels the sun in his eyes. He is safe. He can hear the hunt following him still, but they will not come here. Down the hill he hears his name called over and over. The cries are thin.

He begins to breathe more easily. He looks about him and there is his uncle's jacket folded on a fallen branch. There is the slash-hook, the stack of blocks, the axe. On the trunk of an ash-tree he sees the chainsaw, it's teeth jammed in a raw cut. A spread of dry shavings and sawdust.

But what if his uncle has gone home for the dinner?

What if they know that and in the present silence are approaching through the dark wood? What would they do to him? They had told him before. They usually waited at the beginning of their road, he had grown to expect them. He was relieved to find no one there this time; but they were waiting in the wood, the shortcut home. He thought they wanted to call him names, as they always did. But they could call him names outside on the road. No need to hide that. Today there is more. If he is alone here, they will get him.

He looks around for a weapon but before he can make up his mind he hears their feet in the dried leaves on the perimeter of the clearing. Three of them have followed him.

We found you, Tommy. Take it easy, lad. We're not going to ate you.

Their fists hang relaxed. One carries a stick casually stuck under his armpit.

He tells himself that they aren't going to kill him. They only want to get him because he lives in Ashgrove Park. If he can face them, he will survive and that would be the end of it all. He had only run away in the first place because he knew there was a chance. He had heard the chainsaw from the wood and guessed it was his uncle. If he can face them now, he might get away lightly, or his uncle might come back.

Then he sees his uncle coming out of the trees, buckling his belt. He stops in mock astonishment, then winks at them.

Howye lads?

He grins and jerks his thumb back at the woods but says nothing. They all look at each other.

Want a shot at the axe? He hefts the axe and leans its handle towards Tommy. Have a go, Tommy boy.

Tommy takes the handle. The shiny head seems to drag him down and he is ashamed that he can't lift it. He looks around and sees their faces looking at him, all their jeering gone. Now they look worried. One of them spits. And they are always spitting. So Tommy lifts the axe and brings it down with force to cut a short trench into the soil. When he drags it out, it is smeared with reddish leaf-mould.

There's a great swing to it, Uncle Pad, he says. He feels like winking except that he doesn't know his Uncle Pad very well.

Good man, says Uncle Pad.

He notices now that they are leaving, one by one. Good luck so, they call and shift back into the trees.

When they are gone, Tommy sits down on the tree-trunk with the sawcut three feet from him, the chainsaw protruding like a huge handle. He sees a leak of slime where the blade meets the body. His knees feel wobbly and his head is light.

After a time he remembers that he is also afraid of Uncle Pad, that he is a rough man who drinks porter and urinates on the street. That his father had forbidden Uncle Pad the house five years ago and had only relented when Pad got married and wanted to bring his wife on a visit. She was a thin-faced woman who slipped a 50p into Tommy's hand and pinched his face as she was leaving. She was a piano teacher and his mother had argued with his father about whether or not he could go to her to learn music.

Pad picks the axe out of the earth. You put the shite crossways in the buggers, ha?

He looks Tommy up and down slowly. Tommy wonders what he might be thinking. He stares at the bushes on the other side of the clearing for so long he feels tears behind his eyes. He dreads that he might give way. His mother has told him not to be afraid to cry, but he didn't think Uncle Pad, who is his father's brother would agree. Although his father doesn't actually disapprove of crying, Tommy has never heard him approve of it either. And Uncle Pad is never mentioned at home now.

Come here, I'd put muscles on you. Here stand up. Square up like this. He spreads his legs and stiffens his arms. I'd lay them out.

Ah, Uncle Pad, I'm no good at that. At all.

Pad laughs. He reaches forward and grips Tommy's arm, dragging him to a standing position. He takes his forearms and tilts them at the correct angles. He straightens Tommy's shoulders. His grip is terrible.

Tommy, he says, I'm going to make a man out of you, that your dad couldn't do. You'll only thank me for it.

Tommy smiles weakly.

Suddenly Pad darts the flat of his hand to land on Tommy's cheek. Surprised, Tommy ducks in time to meet a second one swinging in lower down. Now the blows come quickly. One, two, three, four. Pause. His head is noisy. Pad is smiling at him.

How's that feel, ha? Shaping up now, ha?

My head feels sore.

All in a day's work, lad. The fist darts again, closed this time. It strikes Tommy on the shoulder and pain roars in his neck. He cries out. Pad laughs loudly. Move! he shouts. You have to move, boy. Get on and dance!

Tommy steps backwards but Pad follows, his fists darting still. When Tommy tries to ward the next blow, it strikes him on the wrist. He hardly feels it. The next takes him in the stomach and knocks the breath out of him. He doubles, gasps and keels over onto the dry leaves. He can hear Pad's laughter. He hears the rasping of the leaves and feels his uncle's hand on his back.

Pad rolls him over and begins to remove the sticks and earth from his hair. Are you alright, boy? I only meant fun. We all need a bit a hardship.

Tommy nods. He is terrified and doesn't want to draw more on himself. He thinks he should get up now and say thank you for the lesson and walk off into the woods. He thinks that was the kind of thing his uncle would expect. Later he would tell his mother and she would tell his father. But instead of getting up he tries to lie as still as he can, his arms locked over his stomach, his face fixed in a smile.

Pad smiles too. I'd say that was alright, ha? The oul bit of shove? Where did I hit the last wan? He takes Tommy's hand away from his stomach and lifts his shirt. There is a red patch on the lower rim of his breast-cage about the size of a sycamore leaf. Pad touches it. He licks his lips.

It'll maybe bruise. He doesn't seem sorry. Don't say a thing to your daddy now?

Tommy shakes his head.

That's good anyhow. You're a tough little bugger right enough. Won't be long till you're man enough for them bastards.

He says nothing for a while, then he reaches down quickly and catches Tommy in the groin and squeezes. Tommy cries out again and doubles over on his side. He feels his whole torso contract and vomit rise in his throat. He is crying now, unable to control the tears.

Eventually he draws his knees up under him and gets up. Pad watches him coldly from a squatting position. He spits into the bushes. Not a word, right?

Again Tommy shakes his head. He gets up and walks towards the path. He looks at his uncle with hard bright eyes, pinched with pain. Pad looks away.

If you meet the bastards give them what-for, like I done. Come up here again tomorrow, Tommy boy, he shouts.

Once into the shadows Tommy feels safe. He can hear the voices of the others below him in the laurels. They are waiting for him to come back.

Before he gets down that far he hears the chainsaw splutter and scream into the wood. He notices that his fists are clenched tight.

SIGNALS

When his turn came Uncle Joe sang 'Vilia'. He lifted himself out of his chair, spread his hands and arranged his face in an expression of operatic pain. It exhausted him. His face greyed over, like the seafront windows, and he sank back again and seemed to vanish into the cushions.

The summer before the letters began to arrive, little blue squares on the lino of his hall, mottled with crab-writing. I was his favourite niece and he had sworn me to secrecy, not about the letters in particular, but about all his goings-on. But these were the only letters he never mentioned to me. All the others were manila, franked in London, from various branches of the Exchequer. He was in constant communication with the Inland Revenue in respect of his Navy pension. He planned every letter like a battle or a triumph, saving up vituperous comments like rare stamps. *I faced the muzzles of The Bismark and delivered guns to Old Joe Stalin to protect the right of fools to enter civil service examinations,* or simply, *Long division seems to be beyond you, yours sincerely...*

Here Peg, he would say to my mother, what about this then?

It would be a slip of paper torn from a Capital Jotter that he always kept handy. Later, written fair on Basildon Bond, he would hand it to the postman or slip it into the post-box, cursing darkly under his breath.

This, he would tell anybody who passed, is for the you-know-whats!

If they stopped, he would inform them that it was a sad day for the English workingman when old Clem Attlee got his hooks in them. Then every morning for weeks he would prop himself against my mother's sink, blocking the light from the one cavernous window, and worry about the silence from London.

My mother had grown used to these outbreaks. He had been at war with England ever since the day, ten years before, when he came swinging down the gangway of the Inisfallen with a filthy kitbag over his shoulder. He hugged my mother, shook hands with my father and hoisted me into his arms and over his head, calling me his Colleen Bawn, telling me I had his hair. He was six feet six inches tall and his eyes were as pale as shells. Then he put me down on the dock and turned to the disgorging boat. That's the last bit of John Bull I'll see for a spell, he said. The Inisfallen turning down the harbour for the open sea has always been John Bull since then.

G.B.S., he told me later. *John Bull's Other Island*. Old G.B.S. was a better man than Shakespeare. G.B.S. was a politico, but your man Orwell put a stop to that. It did no good for the Reds to have books about pigs written about them.

And then there was Paul Robeson, which generally brought things round to Gigli, McCormack, Tito Gobbi, Richard Tauber, Nelson Eddy,

Joe's language was exotic to me, spattered with Englishness or Navy words. Washing was *dobeying*, a new suit was *shipshape and Bristol fashion*. When he was hungry he would call for *cooks to the galley*. Most women were *My Dear*, and when he shook hands he said *How do you do*, or *My pleasure*. All his letters were *signals*.

Stand by for Mr Peter Dawson, baritone, he told me the first time I saw the little blue envelopes, I'll read the signals later.

Mr Peter Dawson revolved at 78 rpm under the gantry of the windup gramophone — 'Afton Water' or 'Linden Lee'. It was the morning concert — two songs and a cup of tea in the hand, the summer gathering impetus outside. Small boats thudded companionably. The bay gleamed like steel. Inch by inch the sun came round to fall in a bright triangle on the lino, the neat hall with the empty bamboo whatnot, the cardinal-red skirting boards glowing in the dark. Ceremonious as always, he showed me to the door and stood gazing out towards the shipping in the roadstead.

Uncle Joe, do you ever want to go back to sea at all?

He laughed and jerked his thumb at the graveyard looming through the trees on the hillside.

Well, Vanessa, he said, half my chums are up there and the other half are in Davy Jones. You can get enough of a good thing.

So I didn't tell anyone about the letters. It was a secret Joe and I saved — along with lemonade bottles full of poitín that he drank with milk and kept in the case of the wall-clock, and *The News of The World*, borrowed for the sport. They were intimacies, precious and binding. But my curiosity was roused. And when I saw more letters arrive, almost two a week, and when he didn't say anything about them, I became determined to find out for his own good.

One evening we sat in his front room, the late sun warming us through the glass. He had an unseasonable cold and was holding a warm tot of poitín in his lap. Every few minutes he would crumble and wheeze and afterwards his breathing would sound like someone tearing paper. I was idling through the albums of old postcards and photographs his mother had kept. All his ships' tours were there: *China Station 1936* or *Crossing the Bar: The Arrival of Neptune*, a hoary god that was Uncle Joe in the bow of a twelve-oar cutter, or *Testing the Tubes*, a snub torpedo leaping at the sea. He was there in most of them, jaunty, loose-smiling, long-headed, his sailor's blues and his saucepan hat. I thought he was the most handsome sailor I had ever seen. He laughed at that. A girl in every port, he said and winked. But only one Colleen Bawn!

Why didn't you marry at all? I asked.

I was often married but never churched. He tapped the side of his nose and winked.

I had suspected that. In an instant I imagined a career of debauchery that crossed three continents and forgave him for it. I knew now what the signals were. Recriminations or appeals, begging letters, frustrated curses, love-letters. Love-letters that he would not answer. They came twice weekly and nothing but terrible judgments addressed to the Inland Revenue went out.

I began to worry that he was throwing away a chance of happiness in his last days, probably because of what the village might say. I pictured her as a blond, buxom Englishwoman, who had loved him first as a sailor, who had a baby by him during the war while he froze on a convoy to Murmansk. Afterwards, wayward, he refused to be tied. He rejected her. She had, perhaps, tried to kill herself but had been saved by neighbours with handkerchiefs over their noses to filter the gas from the open oven. She pulled herself together in that English way and settled down, in Hammersmith or Woking, to take in other people's washing. She was respectable now, over the other side, her little boy grown up, but would arrive on the half-four bus from Cork like a flying bomb.

I knew of course that I would stand by him should such a harridan turn up on his doorstep after all these years, shoving her nasal English into our soft brogues. I would defend her throughout East Cork, to my friends at school, to the bus driver who delivered her, to my father's relations. I steeled myself for the day when his answer would go out, when the village would take arms against us.

All through August, lying between the rocks on Corkbeg Strand, I listened to the tinkling shells along the waterline and thought of disaster. The pregnant sky, the heat, the volatile clouds all seemed to presage. All this is too good to last, I thought. This happiness.

Instead of war the autumn gales came early, the sky came down, the boats were taken up. Spray lashed the windows of our houses. People going to the shop held onto their hats and made little rushes between waves. The tides came up the sewers. Dogs coursed rats behind the quay wall.

One night my mother heard his gramophone crackling over the wind in the small hours. She called my father and they went to investigate, mackintoshes tied over night-clothes. They found him sitting by the dead fire, wrapped in blankets, the gramophone by his side, the crank in his hand.

My mother was white-faced as she rang the doctor. She held the phone rigidly against her ear and I noticed the whiteness of her knuckles. I think he's after having a stroke, she told me. But it wasn't a stroke. The following morning we drove him to the Regional Hospital. Wind screamed through my father's old Escort, rain blotted out the windscreen. Over the rattling engine I heard my parents hushed voices and Uncle Joe muttering and telling stories. He seemed happy, but all his gallantry and bravado was out of joint, somehow disconnected from himself. At Midleton he fell asleep briefly, woke to tell me a story but lost track halfway through and said, I'll wear no poppy!

In bed later, with the grainy sheets drawn up to his chin he said, Good lads all. Good chums. I seen them in a sea of oil. Oil on troubled waters, Peg, he said to my mother.

That's right, Joe, my mother told him. Rest now. Have a nice rest for yourself.

I saw my father slip a bottle of Paddy, a tiny one, into the top shelf of his locker.

Have I a mug for me choppers? Joe asked. When his teeth were out, his face looked empty and anonymous.

My mother gave me the key to his house. I was to warm it up – light the fire, dust the shelves, air the bedroom and wind the clock. She told me, lying I think now, but for my sake, that he was expected home, that he would be alright soon.

And I did light the fire, then mooned through the rooms staring at hovering motes. The sun had come out again, but incensed by the storms it was glassy, betokening winter. I cranked the gramophone—Mr. John McCormack circling through 'Oft in the Stilly Night' and 'The Croppy

Boy'. Then 'Vilia', 'Linden Lee', 'Afton Water', 'Ben Bolt' and 'The Harp that Once', all the nostalgia of stiff collars and genteel thank-yous.

Over the mantelpiece was a photo of his grandparents taken on their wedding day, romantically brooding at each other before a photographer's landscape of Greek Columns and storm-clouds, intensely pale, sepia hair still un-greyed. The music swirled around them like wind, not altering them. Without knowing I was looking, I found his blue letters in a box in a cupboard under dusty folds of *The News of The World*. They were tied with a brown shoelace. They were unopened. I held them in my hands and stared until furious tears scalded my eyes. It was all over. I opened the knot and put them one by one into the fire. They puffed up and cracked as the flames licked through. Sometimes I could see the writing — mahogany in the heat — inside the crumbling shells. And then all that was left of them was a delicate structure of carbon, oscillating briefly in the downdraft.

They sent him home for Christmas. We put him in our back bedroom and he never once asked for music. He smoked John Player's and at night I could hear spasms of coughing. I suggested cough syrup and he laughed and jerked his thumb upwards: The boilers are blowing! he said. On Christmas day he sang for us, struggling out of his chair. He spread his hands and filled his chest and when he opened his mouth the flesh tightened along his cheeks. Vilia, o Vilia, witch of the wood! How I would die for thee, dear, if I could. His lungs creaked like a dying ship, and because he was singing and dying, and because of the letters he never read, I almost fell in love with him again.

BRIDEY AND JIM ON KODAK

In 1955 or '56 she was standing outside the old square-towered church in Inch, her white dress and handbag, the veil that could not disguise the delight in her face. The brown plaster provided the contrast, gave the tiny photograph a slightly luminous quality. To each side and slightly behind stand her parents, beaming openly; behind those again her brothers' thin faces and tight suits, short hair, the ghost of a Woodbine still in their mouths.

The photographer was an aunt, fumbling over the Kodak box camera, stepping back and back to get them all in the frame. Press the button, then crank the handle to wind the film on.

Jim wasn't there. The delay over the photograph infuriated him, a bad sign on a wedding day, so he was in Mac Carthy's snug with the golden swirl of a large whiskey in his palm, talking hurling. Some time later, when the wedding party missed him, a boy was sent to call him to the church. Gerry Winton was waiting in the big black Zephyr wedding car to drive them home. By then the photographic aunt was tired and weeping. And so it is that his memory is perpetuated only in the words on a grave stone, not in the durable stock of light and shade, the product of the composing eye.

Of course there are chance appearances in other people's photographs, nothing significant, never enough to flesh out his features. The half-face deep in shadow at the back of a crowd at a hurling match (Inch beat Glounthane 2-7 to 1-9). Or he is the cloth cap pulled well down over the eyes just to the left of the lorry from which some politician was speaking. Behind him is the line of loafers that waited every morning after mass to watch the women and smoke. Waifs and strays, these old photos, neighbours will burn them during a spring-cleaning, or they will end their days fluttering like migrant birds at the edge of a County Council tip.

That was the year the oil refinery started. Money and American engineers flooded in. Most of these 'visitors' had nowhere to stay, so women rented out their bedrooms for more than their husbands made in a week. Every man in Inch had a job, the construction work soaked up every available labourer. Farmers complained there was no-one to pick potatoes. It was boomtime. The shops stocked peanut butter, sneakers and DC Comics. The pubs got Southern Comfort and Jack Daniel's.

Bridey and Jim were renting a cottage that belonged to the butcher and Bridey always associated paying the rent with the smell of well-hung meat.

A week after they were married an American offered to pay twice as much as their rent, if they would let him have a single room to sleep in. Bridey said no and Jim said yes. Bridey said she wanted her privacy. Privacy was important to people like her. Even in her father's house she had always had her own bedroom, though her four brothers slept top and tail in two double beds in one room. Now she didn't want anyone else around the place, this was the only honeymoon she would have.

Jim had no concept of privacy. He never left the door closed when he pissed. In fact he was happier pissing in the yard when the weather was fine. He had a rim of grey-brown around his torso where he stripped his shirt off to work. Dirt was ingrained in his neck and in the ripples of his muscles. Bridey knew she should find those muscles attractive, but all they did was frighten her. She thought she should not be disgusted by the sight of her husband making water in the dandelions behind the house, but it made her tremble with disgust.

The American moved into the spare room three weeks after the wedding. By then she was terrified that he would hear what went on in their bedroom at night. Although she had tried everything, she could not prevent the springs and the bedframe from screeching. She was prepared to put up with the pain and the indignity of the process if only there could be less noise. She was sure it could be heard on the street on quiet nights, the way she had once heard Jim breaking wind as she approached the door of his mother's house. She imagined people gathering on the street to hear Jim's wordless passion driving into her.

The American was called Henry J. Winter. He tried to get them to call him Harry, but she could never refer to him as anything but Mr Winter.

In many ways, having Mr Winter in the house was as bad as having Jim. He was always up early so that she lost the quiet minutes alone when the kitchen was hers. He was there at breakfast and the memory of Jim's fumbling and portery sex was in the air between the three of them. There was no complicity in it, it was like a threatening fog. They ate their rashers in silence while she fried bread. Mr Winter drank Irel coffee until she was able to get instant. Jim poured porter-thick tea and clanked his spoon in the cup. He left the spoon in while he drank, so that his drinking was combined with the slight sudden scrape of steel on china. She served the fried bread and their knives scraped on the plates. Mr Winter always thanked her and left early. Jim listened to the radio until he was already late for work then went out without a word.

Jim was working on the construction and across the way Bridey could see the trees coming down, the concrete going in, the steel tanks rising like hard round torsos on the little island. A jetty was stretching out from the island to deep water, where future ships would dock and discharge their crude oil. Offices were rising on the hill, square, concrete and glass buildings such as she had never seen before.

She remarked on these buildings once to Mr Winter and he told her that all the buildings were like that Stateside. The phrase remained with her. It seemed to her that he came from a land of square houses and huge expanses of concrete. She pitied him and yet she was in awe of him. He was a foreigner and she had never met a foreigner until she met him.

He did not often talk of home and seemed to have no homesickness, a kind of rootlessness that appalled Bridey. On the other hand, he went away most weekends in his sharp nosed Anglia and toured Ireland. He came home with stories of places she only knew from her primary school geography—Killarney, Dingle, Kilkee, Galway, Wicklow. Sometimes he posted cards to her—Hi Bridey and Jim, I'm in Dublin. Inch is better. See you Sunday night. Pointless messages that troubled her with their suggestions of escape and other modes of existence.

By contrast Jim was proud of them and often showed them off to his friends. He kept them in a drawer in the bedroom press. And though he liked the cards, and liked to use American expressions like *ain't* and *darn*, he pretended to despise the newcomers. Still he used to lecture her about the money the Americans were making on the construction, and about how they spent it as fast as they got it, about how they were all feckless wasters.

Bridey never sought Mr Winter's attention, but in time she became aware that he was attracted to her. It would have been the most natural thing in the world to take him into her bed some evening when Jim was out drinking. Jim would never have been sober enough to notice and he came home as regular as clockwork at closing time, went straight out into the back yard to relieve himself and then fumbled into bed. But this was 1959 and anyway Bridey did not have a high opinion of sex. What little she had of it had been painful, tense and predictable and it left her with no desire for more. But she did enjoy the attention. She let him watch her as she made the breakfast, especially in the early morning before she called Jim, the quiet ten minutes when she and Mr Winter were alone in the kitchen and the rashers, or bacon as he called it, were sizzling in the pan. He frequently complimented her on her appearance, a thing Jim had stopped doing after she agreed to marry him. Often he offered to help her but she refused, telling him that he was their lodger and he was paying her. Just saying it gave her a curious, nervous pleasure.

There is a photograph of Bridey and Mr Winter, standing with their backs to some fuchsia bushes in bloom. The naked pink legs of the fuchsia under short skirts forms an erotic backdrop. His arm is around her shoulders in a brotherly fashion and she is clearly uncomfortable. She has said something to him which has made him smile, and she is pushing away slightly, turning towards his body as she does so. His is a tanned open face with baby-pale eyes. He has an extremely thin tie and his jacket has broad squares of an indeterminate colour, because this is a black-and-white snapshot, product of Kodak.

But who is the photographer? One of the other engineers or draughtsmen from the site? The photograph was developed in Barry's of Cork. Another snap from the same lot shows the gleaming tanks on the island. Moored at the end of the jetty is the black hull of an oil-tanker, unnaturally canted upwards out of the water like a breaching whale. There is something bleak about the light, as if the atmosphere of that bleak decade has got into the developing chemicals.

By then the construction was over, the Americans had moved on to some desert or sea-borne platform, some other village where there would be other women with spare rooms. The American money, however, had been put to good use. Bridey had a green formica kitchen and a brown formica table. She also had an Electrolux washing machine that washed clothes while she stood over it, occasionally adding soap or reaching in with a wooden tongs to lift the gleaming fabric from the suds. She was beginning to feel that there was not such a huge gulf between Inch and America after all.

The world is full of pictures of Inch during the construction, snaps scattered all over the earth, wherever Shell Oil went, or even in the Bronx and Manchester. The ghostly shapes of cranes and pile drivers, those ancient rounded Caterpillar tractors, the gantry rising in cross-tree'd steel above the head of the jetty. Neat American homes with front lawns without hedges, newspapers lying at the front door in the early morning; their walls are lined with testaments to Ireland's first and only venture into petroleum self-sufficiency. How many of those snaps show Bridey standing at her front door, sitting on the wall watching the sparkling sea? Based on an educated guess, perhaps less than one percent.

Mr Winter never took her picture. Perhaps he got a copy of one taken by a friend. Perhaps he carefully manoeuvred the camera so that a shot of the sun setting over Cobh had the cathedral spire like a pin pricking an orange balloon—so that Bridey's shadow lay across the foreground. Perhaps she appears on the edge of the field, hauntingly unfocussed. Perhaps he did not use the camera to filter his memories. There are people like that.

And the small rooms in the Bronx where one-time players in the Inch Hurling team huddle over their electric heaters and cans of beer? The photographs lie at the bottom of drawers full of payslips and pink slips, old Greyhound bus tickets, the detritus of a life lived so close to the edge of destitution that there is nothing to write home about.

In 1961 Mr Winter moved on to the next Shell project. The latest thing, he told her, was undersea oil, and he would be working for a time on setting up a floating oil-factory someplace. Or else, he said, he would be sent to Nigeria. The day he told her he was leaving he also told her about the majestic wasteful burnings that occur where the oil breaks the surface, how the oil companies keep the price up by delaying ships at sea for weeks on end, how oil in the North-African deserts just leaks out into the sand. He told her about the beauty of the engineer's work, the delicate balance of rate of flow, viscosity, temperature, combined with the simple elegance of steel, the glorious violet flame of the welders.

He did not ask her to come with him. They were already long past that point, if the point had ever existed. Instead he showed her that there never was anything but the briefest contact between her world and his, and she understood exactly what he was saying.

He said good-bye in one of those early morning moments delineated in her memory by the sensual odour of frying bacon, by the hissing silence and the clatter of a pan, by sunshine through the net curtains, by the firm pressure of his hand on hers. She kissed him on the lips, momentarily maddened by the light and his proximity. He looked into her eyes and she could see he was not happy. Then they heard Jim's boots clattering on the bedroom floor and Mr Winter sat down to his breakfast.

Two years later Jim was working in the refinery. He was getting up late and leaving early, the pint pulled him like long hawser at the jetty. Apart from that he was steady and dependable. He never missed a day and he was ready and willing to do any work. His job involved climbing up on the tanks and walking over the lid. This lid was designed to float up and down as the oil-level in the tank rose or fell. He was specifically instructed not to wear boots with toe-caps or hobnailed boots, not to smoke, not to carry anything metal that might fall and cause a spark. So long as he observed those simple precautions there was no danger whatsoever. The problem was that gas accumulated between the surface of the oil and the floating lid.

In July 1963 Jim wore his old labourer's boots up onto the tank and the tank exploded. In the process it exploded Jim's body like a manufacturer's diagram. It blew the lid upwards and the lip of the tank outwards and a spectacular jet of flame shot several hundred feet into the afternoon sky. Most of Jim was blown clear of the flame and so searchers were able to collect about sixty percent of his body for burial. Bridey wore a black dress and a black handbag and her brothers carried the coffin, scarcely noticing the weight. Her parents were dead, and so could not take their place in the arrangement. Besides, in 1963 no one took pictures of funerals.

ETTY FITZ AND JACK CROWE

E tty had tall hair that built up like a picture of the Empire State Building and stopped at a gleaming tortoise-shell comb. She always looked stern. Her faced was whited out by powder and then lined again with eye-liner where her eye-brows should be, mascara to suggest the shape of her eye-sockets, lipsticked lips edged with the care of a portrait artist, rouge indicating cheekbones. Somewhere under this was a skull covered in lined and worn skin. Her lips were sprung on taut wires of disapproval, her eyes supported by a safety netting of creases. Etty had a hard life. She dominated the atmosphere of Fitzpatrick's Bar and Lounge, thriving on the smell of smoke and slops and vomit.

I see her now. She is moving along the street during the holy hour, a net bag on her arm. The net bag contains two cylindrical brown paper parcels, a pound of freshly cut ham, a loaf of Day's bread, and two letters one in a brown envelope and one in a white. The brown paper parcels contain bottles of Buckfast Tonic Wine, to be delivered to the elderly Mrs Simpson, who is an invalid and has been advised to take something for her nerves. Etty will stop and talk to Mrs Simpson who will be sitting in the sunny spot in her hallway this fine summer's afternoon. Etty is returning from the baker's and is beginning to think she should be moving a bit more quickly, opening time being only ten minutes away. Nevertheless she stops and has her chat with Mrs Simpson.

Mrs Simpson struggles out of the depths of her nap to recognize Etty. She takes a blue leather purse from under the cushion she is sitting on and counts out the shillings for the wine. Now she wants to talk about the Americans. She doesn't like them and she thinks the whole idea of a refinery is stupid. Everyone knows, she says, that oil is going to run out in 1990 anyway, and they have taken away the lovely hotel and the golf course that the visitors used to play on, and the lovely ballroom with the maple floor.

That is progress, Etty tells her. You can't have omelettes without breaking eggs.

Mrs Simpson has never made an omelette. The allusion passes her by.

I used to be able to sit here and look at the island and think about all the visitors walking around the hotel. Now look at what they have. She points towards the shiny round tanks of the new oil refinery.

Etty moves on.

The Yanks are good for business. They come into her bar on Saturday nights and play poker and drink whiskey and smoke. Some of them smoke cigarettes and some smoke cigars. Poker has displaced the old games — Forty-five and Hundred-and-ten. Now the locals all know the slang, raising and calling, seeing and smoking, upping the ante. She hears it all over the public bar. There is something offensive about it but she can't quite see what.

She calls at Cleary's shop for the messages and stuffs them hurriedly into the net bag. Now she is striding along the street, rounding the corner into New Line to see the usuals waiting at the door for the moment when they will be released into the comforting cool and darkness of Etty Fitz's.

She has the Yale key ready and at exactly two o'clock she pushes through the door and the smell of home hits her.

Jack Crowe is the worst of the poker men.

When he came first he acted like the nicest man you could meet. He used to snap his fingers and sort of flick his body and say, Join me gentlemen? Meaning anyone in the place for poker? He told stories and cracked jokes and explained the finer points of the game and the different kinds of game you could play. He showed people how to shuffle by holding half the cards in each fist and flicking them together with the thumb.

He drank Jack Daniel's and nothing else. No local customs, he used to say, I'm a down-home boy. The only thing he learned in the two years he was working on the site was the taste of Woodbines. He even picked up the local name for them — Coffin-Nails.

A packet of Coffin-Nails, Etty.

Some of the other Americans only smoked American brands or cigars; he was never seen without a Woodbine hanging from his mouth.

I see him.

He is sitting at the corner table with his chair-back tilted to the wall. There are three farmer's sons and another American at the table. There is a small pile of money in front of each player and a large pile of money in front of Jack Crowe. His face is beaming, the span of his smile only limited by the necessity of holding onto the Coffin-Nail in the right-hand corner, although he has learned the trick of sticking it there with a little drying spittle so that he can talk. His eyes flick from face to face and hand to hand and he is watching their nervousness, aware that as long as he is winning, they will each betray their weakness in their own way. One sweats when he has taken a chance. One sucks air in between a gap in his front teeth. One shifts his backside on the chair. One smiles.

Jack Crowe is always smiling. He talks constantly. Win or lose he always has the latest story. Some of the stories are enough to make the farmers' sons sweat anyway. They are learning about the biological make-up of women and men and the variety of human pleasure, and to two of them the education is worth what they are losing to Jack Crowe. The third is unable to think straight. Aware that once again he has lost the money he was given by his mother to buy beet pulp for the cattle for the winter.

Jack Crowe sits on the ridge of Etty's roof smiling at passers-by and talking through a cluster of nails. He is replacing what he calls the shingles on Fitzpatrick's Bar. The storm has disturbed the ridge-tiles and there is a water stain on Etty's bedroom carpet. When he is not talking he sings. 'Whispering Grass' is his favourite. He cannot say why but he is convinced it is an Irish song and everyone is too polite to tell him otherwise.

Etty is frying steak and onions. She is weeping copiously. Tears stream down her make-up, accompanied by a watery sludge of mascara. She is not weeping because of the onions. She is weeping because her skin is ravaged by age, because she has wasted her life serving drink to farmers' sons who would never marry anyone without land. She is weeping because she has fallen for Jack Crowe and she knows she is not good enough for him. Because he could have the pick of all the girls he has ever seen around the world wherever oil was refined and because he had chosen none. And certainly, if he had not chosen one of them, he would never choose her.

As she weeps she curses herself for weeping. She tells herself to grow up, to dry up because any minute now she will hear the last nail to hang the last slate and he will slide down the roof ladder and land heavily in her backyard.

What happened to Etty Fitz?

She woke up one morning and heard Jack Crowe snoring in the bed. She turned on her elbow and looked at him. She saw his slack face and dark-rimmed eyes. She saw that his teeth were the colour of old wood. She saw that the skin of his neck was peppered with blackheads. She realized that Jack Crowe had never had the pick of all those girls. Not for many a year. She wondered which of them was more the worse for wear, whether maybe he hadn't got the better bargain.

Then she got up and made coffee for him and tea for herself. While the kettle boiled on her ancient Stanley No. 8 range in which the fire never went out, she washed herself at the kitchen sink and then carefully covered the skin of her face. Then she outlined her features with the various necessary instruments, while the kettle gushed steam at the window. She brought him toast and coffee and sat on the bedroom chair watching him rise out of the whiskey-sleep and gingerly swallow the toast.

Jesus Etty, were his first words.

She smoked Player's and he smoked Woodbines. They had their first cigarette of the day together and filled the room with companionable smoke. Then she went downstairs to get the bar ready, while he slept on into mid-morning. He was wakened by the usuals chatting at the door. As they descended into the cool of the bar, he was putting his left leg into his trousers. By the time he was dressed Etty had pulled four or five pints. She had also made up her mind to sell Fitzgerald's Lounge and Bar and move to Cork. She smiled at her own determination, as she heard Jack Crowe slip quietly out by the house door. In less than a minute he was shambling in from the street and making a pretence of saying hello to her. She did not tell him.

The bar was a going concern. The man who bought it from her planned to keep guests in the first floor and live on the top himself. She told him it would kill him, that he would be married to the place night and day. He said there was a boom coming and that when the Yanks were gone, there would tourists. She did not point out that the Yanks were here to build an oil refinery and that once that was built there would be no tourists. By then she didn't care because the money was in the Munster and Leinster Bank in Midleton. She packed her things into cardboard boxes, filled three suitcases and moved into a flat in Wellington Road, Cork. Once or twice people called but she turned them away. She had one of those new intercoms on the front door so no one even saw her face. Jack Crowe wrote to her for a while but when he got no letter back, he gave it up.

The Oil Refinery was finished about 1960 and all the Yanks moved on to the next big job. The boom was over but people looked forward to the time when droves of thirsty sailors would emerge from supertankers to fill the bars and demand strange delicacies from the shop-keepers. Ships did come in, but by the 1960s, crews were small and mostly Filipino or Greek and they were saving their money to send home. They didn't spend much. Jack Crowe never left. He didn't decide to stay either, he just sort of missed the last boat out. He got a job working for Terry Hennessy in the local filling-station, fixing tyres, filling petrol. His experience in the oil industry probably got him the job.

By a curious coincidence the new owner dropped dead at a point-to-point meeting ten years later almost to the day. He was running down a slope towards a horse that had broken its leg and, when he dropped dead, everyone thought he had tripped. So Etty was both right and wrong: the bar gave him the high blood pressure, but it was betting on horses that caused the stroke.

By then Etty was in the Victoria Nursing Home. Jack hated the new owner's guts and, when he heard the story, he went up to Cork specially to tell her.

He asked Terry for the day off and got no reply as usual. Then, half an hour later, Terry just closed the filling station, put up the closed sign and got out of his overalls. They drove off in a cloud of dust which contained the Ford Cortina. Along the way they stopped a few times, because by then a trip to Cork was a big thing for Jack and he wanted to make a day of it. By the second stop he and Terry were supporting each other coming out, each with a lame leg, each lame leg balancing the other, Terry's was his left, where his hip was shortened by a childhood fall, Jack's was his right, his toe swollen with gout. Jack made jokes about their lameness and about his weak liver and the way his bladder didn't hold as much as it used to. He said the smell of petrol and axel grease and car tyres had destroyed his nose for a good whiskey. He said working for Terry was killing him. He said he always knew he should have married Etty because she was his only chance for happiness. He said she was the only woman who truly understood him. Terry just breathed heavily through his nose with a peculiar sibilant rumble.

When they got to the Victoria Nursing Home, Jack straightened his jacket and tie, got the box of Irish Roses from the back seat and made his way up to Etty's room. She was sitting bolt upright in the bed, staring at the door as if she expected him. He noticed immediately that her make-up was completely wrong. All the lines were haphazard and approximate. A fuzz of hair had grown under the line where she liked her eyebrows to be drawn. A fuzz of light hair grew under her nose. Beadlets of moisture refracted the light there so that it seemed her upper lip was encrusted with tiny stones like watch-diamonds. There was too much rouge and too much lipstick. Then he noticed that her eyes didn't move when he came through the door.

He pulled a chair towards the bed and sat down to look at her. He didn't say a word. After half an hour he left again. Terry was sitting in the passenger seat with the door open and his bad leg stretched out on the footpath. When he saw Jack he got out and went laboriously round to the driver's side.

How's old Etty Fitz? He nodded his head towards the Home.

Jack shook his head. She never lost her sense of humour, I guess. She just cracked up about that poor bastard dropping dead. Cracked up. She was asking for you.

Five miles down the road he noticed that he still had the box of Irish Roses in his hand and was suddenly grateful for Terry's silence.

He is sitting on an old car-seat dozing in the sun. His bad leg is stretched out. His face has the yellow of advanced cirrhosis. His hands are folded across his belly which has been very large and is now slack and pitifully diminished. His right hand hangs down at his side with a suggestion of fashionable langour and a Wills'[s] Woodbine is burning down to his fingers. His fly is open and the smell of whiskey could easily ignite the air around him, engulfing him in a halo of flame that would burn brightly and briefly one last time. But the air does not ignite. Jack Crowe sleeps on.

If he wakes he will hear someone telling him that Etty Fitz died in the Nursing Home last night. Her death is in the *Evening Echo* Births and Deaths.

THE MOUNTAIN ROAD

James Casey drove off the top of Rally Pier. His two daughters were on the back seat.

The tide here falls out through the islands and away west. It runs at a knot, sometimes a knot and a half at spring tide. Listen and you will hear it in the stones. This is the song of lonely places. The car moved a little sideways as it sank. And afterwards great gulps of air escaped but it made no sound. I know these things, not because I saw them but because they must have happened. The sky is settling over Rally and the hills. It is the colour of limestone, a great cap on the country. Ten miles out the sky is blue.

I heard it on local radio, suicide at Rally Pier. I knew who it was.

You cannot see the pier from my house. I got up and and put my jeans and jumper on and climbed the hill through heather and stone, to where I could look down. Bees sang in the air. Watery sunshine from a crack in the clouds. When I turned after ten minutes climbing, the whole bay lay before me, the islands in their pools of stillness, the headlands like crude fingers, boats pair-trawling a mile or more apart but connected forever by cables attached to the wings of the giant net. James was on the boats once. He it was who explained all that to me. I saw the police tape on the pier-head, a tiny yellownesss that was not there before. If he left a note what did it say? Suddenly the song came into my head. 'Dónal Óg'. Even as the first words came I knew what it meant for me. You took the east from me and you took the west from me and great is my fear that you took God from me.

When the song was finished with me, I walked back down home. I was accustomed to think of it like that—not that I stopped singing but that the song was done with me. I made up the bed with fresh sheets and put the soiled ones in the washing-machine. I washed out the floor of the bathroom. Why do we do these things when we are bereft? Then I had a shower and put on dark clothes. I got out the bicycle and pumped up the leaking tyre. My father had shown me how to mend punctures but I could not remember now. I still have the same puncture repair kit, a tin box, but now I kept hash in it. Then I wheeled the bicycle down to the gate and onto the road and faced the hill to the house where the dead girls lay.

They closed the door against me when they saw me turn the bend. Cousins make these decisions, but I leaned my bicycle against the wall and knocked and then they had to let me in. Perhaps it was inevitable anyway. People around here do not shut their neighbours out. They showed me into the front room where the two girls lay in open coffins. Three older women sat by them. I did not recognize them. Aunts, most probably. They had their beads in their hands. I did not bless myself. I go to neither church nor chapel and they all knew it. I stood for a long time looking down on the faces. When old people go, death eases their pain and their faces relax into a shapeless wax model of someone very like them. People say they look happy, but mostly they look plastic. But when a child dies, it is the perpetuation of a certain model of perfect beauty. People would say the girls looked like angels. There was no trace of the sea on them, no sign of the panic and fear that bubbled through the ground-up sleeping tablets that their father had fed them for breakfast yesterday morning. According to local radio. His own prescription. He had not been sleeping for months.

When I stopped looking I shook hands with each of the aunts. Nobody said anything. I went out of the room and found the cousins waiting in the corridor. I asked for Helen and was told she was lying down. The doctor was calling regularly all day. She was on tablets for her nerves. She was very low. I was about to ask them to pass on my sympathy when a door opened upstairs. It was Helen herself. She called to know who was there. It's your neighbour, one of the cousins said. She could not bring herself to name me.

Helen came unsteadily down the stairs.

Her hair was flat and moist. She was wearing the kind of clothes she might have gone to mass in, a formal blouse and a straight grey skirt, but she had no tights on. Her bare feet looked vulnerable and childish. She stepped deliberately, stretching so that at each tread of the stairs she stood on the ball of her foot like a dancer. She came down like someone in a trance. I think we all wondered if she knew who she was coming down for. And if she did what was she going to say.

Cáit, she said, is it yourself? Thank you for coming.

Her eyes were flat, too. There was no light in them.

I'm sorry for your trouble, I said, taking her hand. I held the hand tightly as if the pressure could convey something in itself.

Helen shook her head. Why did he do it? she said. Even if he went himself. But the girls…

Helen will I make you a cup of tea?

One of the cousins said that. She was by Helen's side now, she would like to take her arm and lead her into the kitchen. They did not want her going into the front room and starting the wailing and the cursing all over again. Jesus, Mary and Joseph, it would terrify you to hear the things she said. And here she was now talking to Cáit Deane like nothing happened at all. There was cake and several kinds of bread and honey and tea and coffee and a bottle of the hard stuff and stout and beer. The house was provided against a famine. They'd need it all by and by. This is the way things go at funerals.

He always spoke well of you, Helen said.

We were childhood sweethearts, I said.

He always said you should have trained professionally. He said you had a great voice.

I shrugged. I heard this kind of thing from time to time.

He said it was pity what happened to you.

I felt my shoulders straighten. I was fond of him, I said, everybody was.

He said you had terrible bitterness in you.

I moved towards the door but there was a cousin in the way. Excuse me, I said. The cousin did not move. She had her arms folded. She was smiling.

He said you were your own worst enemy.

I turned on her. Well he was wrong there, I said. I have plenty of enemies.

Helen Casey closed her eyes. The only thing my husband was wrong about was that he took my two beautiful daughters with him. If he went on his own nobody would have a word to say against him. But now he cut himself off from everything. Even our prayers. If that man is burning in hell, it's all the same to me. I hope he is. He'll never see my girls again for they're not in hell. And the time will come when you'll join him and no one will be sorry for that either.

One of the cousins crossed herself and muttered under her breath. Jesus, Mary and Joseph. The doorkeeper unfolded her arms suddenly and stepped aside. I opened the door. I was taken by surprise to find the priest outside preparing to knock.

Oh, he said.

Excuse me, Father.

I pushed past him. I noticed that the tyre was sinking again, it would need pumping but I could not do it here. I pulled it to face away. People say I'm cold. A cold-hearted bitch, some of them say. They say such things. The priest was watching me. He was smiling. Most likely he did not know who I was, the new man in the parish. They'd fill him in on the details in the front room with the two dead girls and the old women with their beads. The cousins would know everything. It was how crows always knew there was bread out. First came a single bird, a scout. There was always one. Then they gather. Before long they're fighting each other over crusts. You can knock fun out of watching them and their comical battles in the back yard. But the minute you put the bread out, one of them turns up to check it out and the others follow soon enough. If you dropped dead on your own lawn, they'd be down for your eyes.

I swung into my bicycle and launched myself down the tarmac drive and out onto the road. I turned for the hill down home but that was not where I was going.

I met the car at the place where the road was falling into the valley. There was no question of slipping past. I braked hard and dragged my foot along the road. By the time I stopped, I was by the driver's door and there was a drop of a hundred feet on my left-hand side. He rolled the window down. It was James' brother Johnny.

You'd think the Council would shore that up, he said.

The crows are gathering.

He nodded.

The priest was at the door.

He nodded again. He looked at me silently for a moment, then he said, He could have asked for help, Cáit. You'd have helped him, wouldn't you? I would any day. All he had to do was ask.

Johnny, I said, you know very well I was the last one he'd turn to. And the last one who could help him. And anyway, there is no help.

You could but you would not.

No, I said, I just could not. You know that very well.

Do you know what, Cáit Deane?

I probably do, Johnny.

He looked at me frustrated. You were always the same. You're too sharp for around here.

I shrugged.

My brother James, he said, you destroyed him.

He destroyed himself. I didn't drive him down to the pier.

Why did he do it if not for you? You took him. You took him and you wouldn't keep him and then you left him. Why else would he do it?

I got my foot on the pedal again and faced down the hill.

Spite, I said. He was always spiteful, like a spoiled child.

I launched myself forward and went clear of the car. In a moment I was past the subsiding section. Fuchsia speckled the roadsides with their first bloody skirts. In the valley the last of the whitethorn blossom. The river at the very bottom gleaming like concrete in a field of bog iris. And ahead was the bay and its islands and the vast intolerant ocean.

I chained the bicycle to the stop sign outside the funeral home. The street was a long one that ran into a steep hill; the funeral home, the graveyard and the church were all at the top of the hill so that the dead could look down on the town, and the townspeople when they looked up from the pavement saw death looming like a public monument to their future. People joked that it was the only town in Ireland where you had to climb up to your grave. To make matters worse the funeral home was owned by the Hill family. There were several Hills in the parish and naturally the funeral home was called The Hilton. They say that the only people making money out of the economic crash were accountants and funeral directors. Even the bankrupt had to be buried by somebody. At the door in a plastic frame was a poster with a picture of an anorexic bonsai plant and the words: Our promise to you, Phone ANYTIME, day or night. You will NEVER get an answering machine.

Funeral homes are always cold. There were pine benches in lines like a church. They had been varnished recently and there was that heady smell. It reminded me of my father's boat, the wheelhouse brightwork newly touched up. It was the smell of childhood.

James Casey lay in a plain wooden box at the top of the room. I could see immediately that the brass handles were fake. Someone had examined a funeral menu and ticked cheap. I went to look down on him. I thought I had nothing to say but when I was standing there I had plenty.

You stupid bastard, I said, you stupid murdering fucking bastard.

There was more like that. I surprised myself at the flow of anger, the dam-burst of fury. After a time I stopped because I was afraid I was going to attack the corpse. And then I thought I might have been shouting. No one came but perhaps funeral directors and their secretaries are used to angry mourners. I stepped back and found my calf touching a bench. I sat down.

They'll all blame me, I told him. They already blame me.

Then I cried.

James Casey looked tranquil and unperturbed. In real life he was never like that. After a time I got up. I looked down at him. His eyes were stitched closed because when he was pulled from the sodden car of course they were open. They are not very expert in our part of the world; I could see the stitches here and there. The funeral director knows from experience that the eyes of dead people do not express emotion but he knows that his clients would see fear in them. Nobody wants to look a dead man in the eye. It's bad for business.

Fuck you, I said.

I turned on my heel and walked out. A tiny sigh escaped when I closed the door like the seal opening on an air-tight jar. My bicycle lay on the ground in its chains. They knifed the tyres while I was with James. I was not going to give them the satisfaction of watching me wheel it down the street. I was going to leave it where I found it. Do not slouch, my mother used to say, stand up straight, put your shoulders back. But I slouched just the same. How many years since I first loved James Casey? I pulled my shoulders back but I kept my eyes on the ground. The thought that I had done something unforgivable. It was always there in the dark.

Things come back in the long run, the way lost things are revealed by the lowest tides, old shipwrecks, old pots, the ruined moorings that once held steadfastly to trawlers or pleasure boats. There are no secrets around here.

KINGSLAND WASTE

I spend my evenings looking out on Kingsland Waste. They have parties here at night. They don't start until midnight. And before that sometimes there are couples arguing. I hear every language. Sometimes I wake and think I am at home. They are always building here. A Wimpey crane is parked not far away behind the council flats. The ex-council flats. They're expensive now. There is a flashing white light on the top. Around the corner is a public toilet. It's fifty pence so people just piss against the outside of it. You shouldn't have to pay for something like that. When the wind blows east I can smell it. I don't sleep here. Not because of the reason you're thinking, but because of the ambulances and the police cars. Whenever they drive through this area they turn their sirens on. And there's a guy on a motorbike who goes to work at four am without a silencer. And sometimes there are parties that go on until dawn. Summer is the worst because it's hot and because people stay out late. In the morning there's piss and broken bottles and beer cans round the front door. The Council cleans it, but not on Sundays.

I'm leaning out now. I can't smoke in the bedroom, it's not allowed. If I lean out far enough the smoke blows away on the piss smell. Sometimes

I feel like leaning far enough to fall. But I don't want to die among the broken Heineken bottles. When I die it will be cleaner. A woman goes by dragging a screaming child by the arm. He's not so much screaming as choking. She's not having any of it, I can see. She's tall and fat. She's black and the child is brown. We get all colours here.

Mine is white.

He's in the shower now. My John. He takes forever in there. Washing me off him. At least I'm not paying for the water.

One time I saw a fight in Kingsland Waste. Two men were arguing. Their shouting woke me up but it didn't wake my John. I went to the window and saw that they were standing under the streetlight. It's a small side-street and so not many people go by at that time of the morning. It was three am. I don't know what they were shouting in, it sounded like Latvian. But I don't know any Latvian. One pushed his beer-can in the other's face. Like a fist. He smashed the can into it. I thought I could hear the sound of the can collapsing. It excited me. They were punching each other. They weren't saying anything. After a time, I don't know how long but it felt like a long time, one man ran away. The other man did not follow. His face was bleeding. He tried to wipe the blood with his sleeve and he looked up and saw me. Even though the bedroom light was off, the streetlight was shining on me. I think I saw that he hated me. Men usually do. He looked at me for maybe twenty seconds and then he looked away and shortly afterwards he walked off in the opposite direction to the other man.

This space under my window is really a crossroads. There are three ways to leave it: onto Kingsland High Street, onto Ball's Pond Road or onto Kingsland Green. There is no green on Kingsland Green, just the old Post Office depot and the backs of some warehouses. Unless you count the trees. They are mountain ash. Kingsland Green leads to Boleyn Road. Boleyn Road leads north, I don't know where. So does Kingsland High Street. And of course they lead south too. I started down there. I moved up the hill. If I had my way I would keep moving, follow the Kingsland Road or Boleyn Road. Always following royalty. I'm an immigrant here, like a million others. The places and the names lead you in. We had mountain ash at home. In the autumn the thrushes stripped the berries like machines.

My John is singing. He has a good voice.

I keep all sorts of stuff in there, every kind of shampoo and body lotion and body soap and aftershave and talc. I buy them in Sainsbury's. Razors too. Men's and lady's. It's not easy to get talc now, but some people need it still I suppose. I get it in Sheer Bliss at the corner of Dalston Lane. They get it for me.

He's singing 'All You Need Is Love'. They all know The Beatles. He's also doing the music bits in between the words. 'All you need is love da da dadadaaa all you need is love'. He works in Canary Wharf in international banking of some kind. He is a relationship manager. The Overground has made all that easy now. He takes the Overground, then the Jubilee Line. The trains on the Overground are class. It's just one long carriage. You can take a walk on your way down through Haggerston, Hoxton, Shoreditch High Street, Whitechapel, Shadwell and all the other places. All the way to Crystal Palace where there's no palace. I go in The Kingsland some nights. It's an Irish pub. *Cead míle fáilte, ceol agus craic.* Not many Irish go in there, but one of the barmen knows me. We have chats. Once he said to me, Why not give it up, Claire hah? And I said to him, Jack, if you can show me something else that brings in four hundred quid a day clean I'll do it.

He whistled. Fair dues, he said, I see your point.

Some fine day, I said, I'll stop just like that.

My mother used to say that, he said. Some fine day hah? Those fine days never come.

My John is out now. I can hear him humming and scrubbing himself dry. He comes out naked and it's my job to admire him. There's nothing much to admire but I have to give him the head-to-toe look and go Mmmm. Sometimes that starts them off again and I have to remind them that it would be double. They never like that. The more money they make, the less they want to pay. But if I asked him to give me two hours of his time for the price of one he'd laugh me all the way to Canada Water. But today it doesn't start him off. He's stressed. He told me that before we started. It's the end of the month and he has a project to finish. It's something to do with a hotel in Dubai. Or maybe that's where the meeting is. They have an end of project meeting always somewhere else. I don't really listen. I'm not expected to. He barely looks at me. He pulls his underpants on and then his shirt. It's a white shirt. When he took it off, he laid it carefully over the back of the chair and laid his trousers across the arms. A black and white cross. When he puts his shirt on, he puts his tie on. He stands in front of the mirror in his underpants and shirt and does his tie up with a Windsor knot. Next he puts his socks on. Shirt, tie, underpants, socks. Then he pulls his trousers on and buttons it and ties the belt. Next come shoes which are black, long and pointed and very shiny. I think he spends a lot of money on clothes. Once he came in jeans and they were Armani. He gets his suits made specially for him. He sits down to tie his shoelaces. His shirt stretches over his back and I see again that he is weak, that there is a line of weak flesh around his waist. He is getting fatter. He sits on his arse all day and comes up here after work once a week. That's his exercise. It won't do his heart any good. Despite the cleaning fluids he used in the shower I can detect a faint smell of myself from him. He is sweating too. After sex my sense of smell is acute. It disgusts me. I never have any problem in advance. I do the business. I charm. I want you so bad, I need you, I've been waiting. I lie down and open my legs. I make the right noises. I make my John feel like the king of all Johns. I smoke while he showers. Then I fucking hate him. He makes me sick. I would vomit on him if I could, down the neck of his white shirt, if I didn't think it would ruin the business. I'm a fucking town planner, I want to say. Do you know who designed my website? I did it myself. And I want to say, Sit down when you piss in my toilet, I don't like cleaning up after you. And it would be better if you showered before we fucked. And after you wake up I don't want to hear about your fucking office problems and the bitch boss and the guys who bitch about her and the guys who get the project done first. I keep a knife under the mattress on the side of the bed I prefer to lie on. I keep it for the day when some shit tries it on with me. I know girls who were beaten senseless. Choked. Had things shoved into them. Let them try that here. I'll go to prison for it. I can see blood on my carpet between the window and the bed. A pool of it, thickening. My John straightens and his shirt loosens and I can't see that line anymore and I relax a little. I feel better. I don't want to kill him now. He turns to me. It's as if he sees me for the first time. It's always like this with him.

What are you looking at? he says.

You're putting on weight around the waist, I say.

He laughs. Does it turn you off?

I think of the knife again. But I put my arms around his neck and say, Nothing turns me off about you baby.

I kiss him on the cheek and he squeezes my hands and thrusts them away.

I can't stay, he says, I have a meeting in two hours.

I smile sadly. I was hoping just today...

Sorry love, he says.

He's one of those men who call all women love. He thinks it's polite. The plumber who came to fix my leak did too, except with him it really was politeness. He was a nice man. We had a cup of tea. He was born in Brick Lane, a proper Londoner. One of five kids. Now he lives in Essex. His daughter lives near with his grandson. His wife developed epilepsy after a trauma. It can happen like that he says. Lucky their daughter is strong. He fixed the leak in the outflow that was seeping under the floorboards and blackening them. But the blackening must stay. It can't be undone. The leak is a river bed black in the wood. A wound.

It's always like this. Before they leave. I hope they'll never come back.

My John kissed me at the door. His lips were dry. I don't think he's married. But married is better. They expect less.

I closed the door, turned the key in the lock and put the chain in place. I heard him shut the street door. He would be going for the

Overground at Dalston Junction. Going south to change at Canada Water. I went to the kitchen to make tea. The stain is slowly drying out and turning brown-black. While the kettle boiled I had a quick shower. There is another bruise on my thigh. The bruises turn them on. Some fine day I will kill someone. It might be me. Death in Kingsland Waste. If I ever get old, these will be my memories. Who wants that?

ACKNOWLEDGEMENTS

I am grateful to the following magazines and anthologies in which the stories in this collection first appeared: *Granta: New Irish Writing* (London); *The Faber Anthology of New Irish Writing* (London); *Ninth Letter* (University of Illinois); *The Stinging Fly* (Dublin); *The Dublin Magazine*; *Inkroci* (Milan); *The Rome Review* (Washington); *Silver Threads of Hope Anthology* (New Island); *Bridges* (Telemos Publishing).

'I am Lost in this House' was part of a commission by Cork City Council and Cork City Libraries, and published in *Southward*, the magazine of the Munster Literature Centre. I am especially grateful to the people of the Northside who agreed to be interviewed by me and to the organisations that facilitated those interviews.

WILLIAM WALL is the author of the novels *Alice Falling, Minding Children, The Map of Tenderness* and *This is the Country* (Sceptre), longlisted for the Man Booker Prize; three collections of poetry, most recently *Ghost Estate* (Salmon Poetry); and one volume of short stories, *No Paradiso* (Brandon). He has won the Virginia Faulkner Award, The Sean O'Faoláin Prize, several Writer's Week prizes and The Patrick Kavanagh Award. Longlisted for the Man Booker Prize and The Manchester Fiction Prize. He was shortlisted for the Young Minds Book Award, the Irish Book Awards, the Raymond Carver Award, the Hennessy Award and numerous others. He has received Irish Arts Council Bursaries, travel grants from Culture Ireland, and translations of his books have been funded by Ireland Literature Exchange. He has also received public commissions. His work has been translated into many languages, including Italian, Dutch, Portuguese, Latvian, Serbian and Catalan. He has a particular interest in Italy and is a frequent reader at festivals there. He translates from Italian and has co-presented workshops in translation. In 2014 William was part of the Italo-Irish Literature Exchange, organised through The Irish Writers' Centre, which toured Italy with readings in Italian and English. He was an Irish delegate to the European Writers' Parliament in Istanbul 2010. In March 2010 he was Writer in Residence at The Princess Grace Irish Library, Monaco. He was a 2009 Fellow of The Liguria Centre for the Arts & Humanities. He has received public commissions including The Shadowlands exhibition and book in 2008 in collaboration with artist Harry Moore. He lives in Cork. For more information go to www.williamwall. net.